For Princess Eleanor and for Peter
(who is really very tidy), love
—S.C.

Book I

The Trials of Thomas

Thomas staggered through the clearing gripping one of his arms. "Arrgh," he moaned. Then he collapsed in the grass, kicking his feet in the air and pretending to wrestle with a sea monster. Around him eight of his brothers and sisters clapped their hands or complained, "That's not how it happened!"

Their da had told a particularly good tale last night about a wounded knight who had managed, with his dying breath, to kill a sea beast. The next day the little ones had begged Thomas to act out the story. He did not mind doing this, for it gave him a chance to think about what to do if he

should ever really come face to face with a sea monster, or what to do if he had only one breath left to live. Furthermore, he'd used the request to get his brothers and sisters to promise that they'd follow him to the river afterward.

It was now warm enough to bathe in the river, and Thomas, as the eldest, was in charge of their much-needed summer scrubbing-up. After shushing all arguments about his retelling of Da's tale, he put baby Isabel on her bottom in the middle of the ankle-deep stream and then got busy chasing down several others to get them washed.

From behind him he heard Isabel cry, "Horsey!"

"We left your toy at home, Izzy," he called over his shoulder as he made a grab for his dirtiest little brother, Peter.

"Horsey!" The little girl giggled.

It was a new word for Isabel, who'd just gotten a carved wooden horse from their father. Since she used the word often, Thomas did not bother to look when she laughed and said, "Horsey!" a third time.

It was not until another sister pointed toward

the stream and cried, "There's a knight!" that Thomas turned and saw a great black warhorse coming quickly around the bend of the rocky riverbed. It was bearing down upon his baby sister. The knight on its back seemed to be looking down, not ahead of him where Isabel sat in the shallow water and clapped joyfully.

"Is-a-bel!" screamed Thomas as he let Peter loose and raced toward the riverbed. "Stop!" Thomas shouted at the knight. He waved his arms frantically.

The knight did not look up; instead, he lurched in his saddle and almost fell off.

He can't hear me! Thomas felt his heart tearing in two. He flew toward his sister—but there were boulders and tree roots in the way. He'd never make it in time. She'd be trampled. "Is-a-bel!"

"Horsey!" She pointed. "Me want." Her hands opened and closed as she leaned toward the oncoming animal.

Thomas's shin smacked against a boulder and he went tumbling headfirst over it. He scrambled back up. As he did, he grabbed a stone and hurled it with all his might at the horse, and missed. He was limping now, and he moaned as he grabbed another large stone. He saw his brother Albert and his sister Margaret racing toward Isabel as well. They would not make it in time. His arm arced back and the stone shot forward. It hit the horse on its muzzle.

The horse reared—its big hooves almost above Isabel's head, its mane, as black as midnight, whipping back—and a high-pitched *eeeeeeeeeeeeeeee* split the air.

Isabel's lower lip quivered. She screwed up her face and bellowed a cry of baby-temper that echoed the horse's cry of panic. "Ah . . . *eeeeeeeeeeeeeeee!*"

The knight slipped sideways into the stream, and the frightened animal bolted up the opposite bank—nostrils flaring and eyes rolling. Snorting and stamping, it got tangled in the brambles along the bank.

Thomas bent forward and grabbed at his side. He tried to catch his breath and thought he was going to be sick. A second later, he raised his head and saw his baby sister safe, but bawling big disappointed tears as she turned on her bottom to

watch the horse. Her little hands were still opening and closing—demanding, *Give me.* The knight,
perhaps knocked to his senses by the fall, was
struggling to rise.

Thomas picked his way through the remaining
tree roots and climbed over the last boulders
along the streamside. He was followed by his
brothers and sisters. He swallowed hard and
panted as he told Margaret, "Get Izzy."

Then he paused to get his strength back,
turned, and limped to the knight's side. With Albert's help, Thomas got the knight to his feet. The
man was groggy and holding his head. Thomas
walked him around the scattered boulders to an
especially broad tree root that lifted out of the
bank. There the knight sat down and leaned
against the trunk of an alder.

He was a big man, with a broad chest—broader
than Da's. He seemed to be an all-over mishmash
of browns and reds. His bushy hair was red. His
beard was red, also, and a bit raggedy. It barely
covered a scar or two on his chin. His armor had
rusted. And his laced-up leggings and boots were
covered with brown mud.

Thomas looked into the man's face. "Begging your pardon, sir, are you all right?"

The knight tried to focus on the boy in front of him. "I think so. My head hurts. What . . . happened?"

"It looked like you were asleep on your horse. My baby sister was about to be trampled, so I hit your horse with a stone and he threw you into the river."

The knight swayed as he peered past the boy to the stream, across at his horse in the brambles, and around at the disheveled group of children who had gathered close. One of them carried a squalling, red-faced baby balanced on her hip.

"I must have nodded off," the knight said. "I've been traveling for two days. I didn't hurt her, did I?"

Thomas shook his head. "No. She's screaming because she wants your horse. Whenever she sees a horse, she wants one."

The knight nodded wearily and closed his eyes. A moment later he opened them and tried to push himself up. "I should see to Eclipse," he said. Then he collapsed against the tree.

"I'll do it," said Thomas, already turning toward the stream.

"Stop!" cried the knight. "He's a warhorse. If he's frightened, he might hurt you."

"That's Thomas," a small, particularly dirty child pointed out. "He likes animals."

"Lots of horses come to our house. Da makes saddles," explained an older boy. "My name's Albert."

"Thomas is brave," added another child helpfully.

"Just this morning he got wrestled by a sea monster," whispered the dirty child.

"No he didn't!" said Albert. "He was just pretend—"

"Please," interrupted the knight, raising a hand and halting the discussion so he could watch Thomas.

Thomas splashed across the stream and slowly and calmly approached Eclipse. He made no sudden moves and was careful to stay where the horse could see him. He spoke soothingly, as he might to Isabel when she was upset. It was only a matter of a few moments before Thomas managed to quiet the startled creature. Then he carefully began to untangle the horse's reins from the briars and vines that grew thick upon the riverbank.

Thomas held the reins firmly and continued to talk and cluck to the horse as he led it across the stream. It had lost a shoe in its frightened dash, and Thomas stopped to retrieve the horseshoe from the water. Upon his return, his brothers and sisters moved back from ogling the knight so Thomas had room to tie the horse to the other side of the alder.

"Well done!" exclaimed the knight. "And you've even found the shoe." The knight sat up a bit straighter. He was still holding his head, but he seemed to be doing better. "Your . . . um"—he made a guess indicating the dirty child by his elbow—"your *brother* here tells me your name is Thomas."

"Yes," Thomas answered as he took Isabel from Margaret. Isabel had stopped wailing and was now staring wide-eyed at the great sweating horse standing nearby. Teardrops plopped from her eyes, but a smile was starting on her face.

She looked up at Thomas. "Mine!" she said.

Most of the group around the knight put their hands over their mouths and giggled shyly.

"I'm sorry," said Thomas. "Right now, everything she likes is hers."

The knight laughed and winced at the same time as he forced himself to rise. "I suspect she'll grow out of that. Well, Thomas, you seem to have everything in hand. I've met some of your family, so now let me introduce myself. I am Sir Gerald of Wellsford. I was on my way to the castle with news for the king. But now Eclipse is minus a shoe."

"Da is very clever with leather," Thomas offered.

"He can do anything!" said the dirty child. "Da were at the castle."

"That's Peter," said Thomas, nodding at his littlest brother and adding, "Da was in training once."

The knight turned to Peter. "He was, was he?"

Peter inspected his thumbs, stuck the cleanest one in his mouth, and nodded vigorously.

Thus, the children convinced Sir Gerald to follow them home. They were sure their father could help by fashioning something for the horse to wear until the knight was able to have its iron shoe refit. So Thomas, followed by his still-unbathed siblings, led a grateful, limping Sir Gerald and his horse toward their home. Peter proudly carried the horseshoe.

chapter 2

Thomas's father tended Sir Gerald's horse. By the fireplace in their cottage, Thomas's mother fed the knight fresh bread and milk. Then she left Sir Gerald to be the center of attention among her young ones while she and Thomas prepared a poultice to apply to the lump on the knight's forehead.

He was a *real* knight—or so said Thomas and Ma and Da. The children could see the scrollwork upon the scabbard of his sword, which he had brought with him into the cottage. Da could work designs in leather, but they'd never seen anything this fine before. And in the scabbard was a real sword. They could see that as well.

They'd never gotten a good look at a knight before. A couple of the youngest ones hadn't even been sure such things as knights existed outside of Da's bedtime tales. Peter sidled close again. He plucked at Sir Gerald's arm and asked, "Have you ever been wrestled by a sea monster?"

Sir Gerald laughed and said, "Not of late." Then he told them of fighting with his brave warhorse for the king on the northern borders. And he spoke of how amazed he'd been when Thomas managed to calm Eclipse at the river.

"Oh! Aye, that's our Thomas all over," said Thomas's mother. "He cannot stand for any creature, big or small, to be suffering. Once, he walked all the way to Millford to set an injured gander in the pond, he was that stubborn about it. He'd taken the notion it would be better tended there by the miller."

"It was our own geese that had pecked it," explained Thomas.

"He walks with me to the little house," said Peter. He shivered, adding, "When it's night."

"Me too! He holds my hand," another child told the knight.

"To the privy," whispered Thomas's mother to

Sir Gerald just as she tilted the knight's head back to get a good look at the large bruise that was forming.

Very shortly thereafter, Thomas turned from the poultice preparations. When he did, it was just in time to snatch up Isabel. She had crawled across the floor to Sir Gerald and was about to poke him with a stick.

"Stop that, Izzy!" Thomas said. "No poking."

"That's her sword," said Peter. "You need a sword to be a knight. He's got one," he finished, pointing to Sir Gerald.

"Well, he *is* a knight," said Albert, rolling his eyes.

"And Izzy is not," put in Thomas as he lifted Isabel high to head off an infuriated scream.

Peter leaned against the knight and, looking into Sir Gerald's face, informed him, "Someday, Thomas is going to be a knight."

"Is he?" asked Sir Gerald, who didn't seem to mind Peter's dirt.

Thomas blushed and turned to tuck Isabel into the basket that served as her bed.

Peter nodded. "And he's going to bring home treasure. Real dragon treasure!"

"Our Thomas, a knight! Don't be silly," Albert scoffed, and made a face.

"He is *too* going to be a knight. He told me so!" Peter shouted.

"Da coulda been a knight," Albert said, "if he wanted to. But not Thom—"

"Hush!" said their mother as she bent to apply the poultice of pressed herbs to Sir Gerald's forehead. "Enough of that. We best stop bothering Sir Gerald and get the lot of you ready for bed." She pushed back a strand of hair. "Albert, stop bickering and take Peter outside. Douse him from the bucket and see if there isn't a boy under what washes away."

Later, after outfitting Sir Gerald's horse with a temporary shoe, Thomas's father entered the cottage. Sir Gerald sat at the table and spoke openly with the good man.

The northern borders were overrun, and almost every able-bodied man who could be spared from the King's Company was doing his best to protect the borderlands from invaders. Even some squires, not yet knighted, were engaged in reinforcing the king's ranks. Sir Gerald was riding back to make his reports and to gather more men to post in the villages in the north. "In truth," said the knight, "I can see that you are an honest man, nimble on your feet, strong, and a talented leathersmith. We need men such as you."

Thomas's heart skipped a beat. What was this? Could it be that his father might see service as a knight after all?

But Da only harrumphed good-naturedly and spread his arms to indicate the little ones around him. "And who would tend to my rioting horde? I've nine children now, and the good woman reports we'll soon have another. I do not know what we would do without the help of Thomas and the older ones to tend to the youngest."

" 'Tis true. You've almost a company of the King's Guard of your own!" The knight chuckled. "Still, the children tell me you trained well at the castle." Sir Gerald let Da gather his thoughts a moment, and then added, "And you've Albert and Thomas and the older girls to help your good-wife."

"Aye. I excelled at archery and lance work," Thomas's father replied. "Since I was stout, I could keep the lance couched low and securely under my arm and up against the lance rest, so my mark was true. And I'm as good a horseman as you'll find in these parts. Still . . ." Da shook his head and looked away. "I were never knighted. 'Twere not the need for so many knights then, and . . . well, my da before me was a leathersmith as well, you see. I had a rough go of it against boys from landholding families. Suppose I'd gotten a fancy in my noggin, that's all. Mists and dreams."

"No! No it wasn't, Da," Thomas interrupted, leaping to his father's side. "He'd make a great knight, Sir Gerald. He's very strong. He—"

Thomas's mother turned from the fireplace, where she'd been stirring some broth. "Thomas! I'm surprised at you," she admonished. "You know better'n to interrupt yer elders."

Thomas's father touched his son's arm to silence him. "Son," he said, "it takes more than strength to be a knight. I know."

Sir Gerald agreed, explaining to Thomas and the children, "Much more. Prior to being a knight, most men go through years of training, starting as young as seven. As a page, they must learn about court life and tending the animals. Then, when they've got about fourteen years, they become a squire and learn how to handle a sword, joust, plan a battle, and lead men. Your da, here, has already been through a good part of that training. It's very hard work."

Thomas backed away from the two men. "I'm . . . I'm sorry." And then he got an idea and he couldn't help himself; almost before he knew it, he'd said, "I'm a hard worker! Ask my da. I'd like to learn all those things. I could be one of the king's men."

Sir Gerald smiled at the boy. "I'm certain that you are a hard worker and a help to your father and mother. I've seen that today. But right now we need older . . . ah, lads." The knight glanced back at Thomas's father. "Though I do think the King's Company could use some new boys; our ranks grow smaller every day as we send ever-younger squires to the borderlands. How many years has your eldest son, Albert?"

"Our Albert is not yet twelve," said Da. "But Thomas, he be our eldest."

Sir Gerald looked surprised. "He's your *eldest*

son?" The knight surveyed the group in the room. Albert was still outside with Peter. Even so, several of the children in the cottage stood taller than Thomas. "I hadn't realized that!"

"He's"—Da cleared his throat and leaned in toward Sir Gerald—"on the short side for having twelve years. But he's right enough about being a good helper. He is that. Whilst I'm afraid our Albert hasn't settled down much yet."

"Well," said Sir Gerald, "I *was* impressed by Thomas's handling of everything at the river, as someone so . . . so . . ." Sir Gerald trailed off, unsure what to say.

Thomas's father jumped in. "We don't pay size much mind here. He keeps up with his chores, and I expect no less of him than I do of any of the others. More, actually, what with him being the eldest, and smart and all."

Sir Gerald studied Thomas for a while longer and smiled. "Really, that's *very* good," said the knight. "Then he is not too young to be sent away to study. Hmm . . ."

"I suppose not," said Thomas's father, scratching his head. "Most boys by his age are already apprenticed out, I know. But I've been busy training Albert. Ya see, as rough as he is, Albert's got a good eye for leather. So we've needed Thomas to help with the little ones. His size don't matter here at home."

The knight placed his forearms on the table and squarely faced Thomas's father. "I like what I see in this son of yours," he told him, nodding toward Thomas. "Though he is as short as a page boy of only seven or eight years, mayhap his growth will catch up with him. He's good with Eclipse. If he doesn't make a squire, the castle could still use a good groomsman. I'd like to take him to the castle to be trained."

Thomas's heart skipped a beat or two. All his life he'd heard his father's bedtime stories about living at the castle, and he had dreamed of going there, too. A squire? Maybe—if he was good enough—he could become a knight one day, like Sir Gerald, with a warhorse of his own, and a sword. He could contain himself no longer.

"Yes!" cried Thomas. "Yes! I *ought* to be trained in a profession, Da. And then there'll be one less mouth to feed here."

"Thomas!" scolded his mother, rounding on

him. "The men are talking. Hold your peace, or the only place you'll be going is outside with Peter to get a dousing."

Thomas blushed a deep red. Yet he stood where he was and drew himself up as tall as he could. He bit his lip and held his breath, awaiting his father's reply.

Da hushed his wife and glanced at his son before answering. "He's a good boy, that he is. And you've a reputation in these parts as an honest and hardworking knight. But, begging your pardon, sir, I'm not sure that's a good idea."

"He will learn much at the castle," Sir Gerald reminded him. "He has some natural talents that can be put to use."

"Aye," Thomas's father said. Then he looked down at the tabletop. Finally, he sighed and said, "That's not what's troublin' me. You see, what it comes down to is, I wouldn't . . ." He paused, and in a lower voice added, "What I'm trying to say is, not only has he got his size against him, but he's the son of a . . . Well, I'm only a leathersmith, like my da before me. I don't want my son to be the target of the same—"

"I understand," said Sir Gerald, cutting in. "In

truth, I cannot promise that he won't have a diffi-cult time of it. However, as a knight, I'm allowed to choose whom I will to serve me. You have a fine son. I have seen that he has a good head on his shoulders. He has as much right to be trained as any young person. I can make no promise except this: I will have a care for his well-being, with the hope that one day he will either be knighted or find a good station at the castle."

"Hope," Da whispered, shaking his head.

Then Thomas saw his father glance at him be-fore looking over at Ma. Thomas's mother stood nearby clutching her arms about her chest. He saw her raise her eyebrows and nod faintly at Da. Thomas held his breath, waiting for what would come next.

Da looked thoughtfully at his red, rough hands for a moment, and slowly extended one toward Sir Gerald. "He's got our permission. I may have me doubts, but I would not deny my son his hope."

Thomas whooped! He rushed his father and then his mother, hugging them both.

After this, Albert returned with a somewhat cleaner and pinker Peter in tow. Albert was not

happy to hear the news. "How come he gets to go to the castle? I'm the one with natural talents. I know leather and how to work it. Even Da says so. I'll just end up doing all Thomas's chores now!"

Later—after more talk, and when the youngest ones had been tucked in—Thomas promised he would return home whenever he could to help with chores. And so it was with much joy that Thomas rode off that very evening behind his new master to the castle.

chapter 3

At the castle, Thomas curled up with several younger boys on a wide rush-covered shelf that dropped from a rough plastered stone wall. Despite his age, he'd been placed with the younger pages in the sleeping loft. Through the darkness he could just make out a patch of timbered roof way above him. The room was much larger than the sleeping loft at home. It felt vast and cold. Still, Thomas smiled to himself—here he was, a leathersmith's son, in training at the castle. He was sure he'd have some marvelous adventures soon—much better than simply acting out Da's stories.

Earlier, on his way up to the sleeping loft, Thomas had passed tapestries hung along the gallery from the great hall. These large hangings held worlds of exquisite knots and delicate stitches depicting all kinds of animals and people and buildings. They'd fairly taken Thomas's breath away. Ma had never made anything like those. He'd wanted to run his fingers over the threads, but instead he'd been whisked away up the steps. Tomorrow he'd inspect them again.

Tonight it was simply too exciting to sleep.

Uh-oh! What was that? Thomas yanked his foot up. Something had just scurried through the grasses on the bed and leapt across his foot. A mouse? Here in the castle? Surely there were cats in the castle to keep the mice away. At home the cats would have made short work of any mice foolish enough to get inside the cottage. Tentatively, Thomas stretched his leg down, but he didn't have long to think about the mouse. From a pallet on the floor, a small boy suddenly cried out.

Thomas dropped down and crossed the short distance to the child's side. The child told Thomas he'd had a bad dream, so Thomas patted his back until the young one fell asleep again. Finally, Thomas yawned and climbed up to his bed on the shelf. Soon he'd make sure he was placed with the older boys. Mice or no, he burrowed down into the prickly rushes, pulled a thin blanket over himself, and fell asleep.

The next day Sir Gerald rode off again to the northern border. The tutors and masters of instruction at the castle took one look at Thomas and assigned him for exercises, work duties, and studies with the much younger boys. Or they almost overlooked him altogether.

When Thomas tried to explain that he was older, he was either laughed at or cuffed about the head for speaking without being told to. His first full day at the castle was not at all as he'd expected. He spent most of the day learning how to serve visitors dining at the lower tables in the great hall. How to bow. Whom to serve first. Where to stand. What to say if asked a question. When to back away. Serving at table was a chore done by all of the pages so they could observe the manners of their betters.

As the days passed, boys his own age or older

avoided Thomas. When their paths crossed, Thomas tried to be friendly. What he got in return were sniggering remarks about what a little pet he was or jibes about the stunted growth of the peasants. No one believed he had as many as twelve years. Thomas fumed, but he did not complain. He learned not to speak up after being reprimanded repeatedly by studies masters and head servants whenever he did so. He kept quiet and spent his days among the young pages.

Truthfully, Thomas enjoyed the pages—they reminded him of his brothers, and of home. At night they would eagerly gather around his bed to hear one of Da's stories. However, he did fear that he'd never get to do anything more daring than serving up trenchers of roasted meat or helping to push around the huge sand-filled barrel that was used to clean chain mail placed within it.

When the weather was good, the games master held sprinting contests for the pages along the length of the castle gardens. Whichever boy finished first, when racing from the rose bower to the king's mulberry tree and from thence to the espaliered apple trees along the kitchen garden wall, could have first choice of serving duties at the lower tables. Since he was older, Thomas usually finished well ahead of the others. But one day he'd just rounded the mulberry tree and was taking his time loping along the path to the kitchen garden when someone whizzed past him.

A real race! Thomas laughed and lengthened his stride. Ahead, the boy who'd passed him was not one of the pages whom Thomas had met, or even one of the younger squires. His hair was curly and tangled, and his clothes bore a number of patches. He must be new to the castle. Thomas smiled. Now he was no longer the newest boy here.

Thomas was almost at the brick wall that encircled the kitchen garden. He was gasping for air and had managed to close much of the distance between them when the boy suddenly turned with an apple in his hand. Shocked, Thomas stopped in his tracks and almost fell over. Apples *were not* to be taken from the trees; they were for the kitchen.

"Hey!" squeaked Thomas. He shakily pointed a finger at the boy to warn him, but first he had to bend down to catch his breath. When Thomas raised his head again, the boy was gone! He was not on the path back to the rose bower. He'd simply vanished.

The very next day, Sir Gerald returned to the castle. With a little instruction from the knight, Thomas fed, curried, and brushed Eclipse. The large horse seemed to like Thomas's touch, and Thomas stayed as late as he could in the stables. Other than the king's warhorse, Heartwind, and a few other beasts—including some ponies and the castle's old donkey, Bartholomew—there were not many animals being stabled. Most were away with the knights at the border.

Thomas leaned his head against Eclipse's side. The stables were a quiet spot amid all the hubbub of the castle grounds. Thomas liked the smell of new hay and oiled leather that lingered there.

Suddenly a laugh rang out. Then an angry shout. The shout, Thomas knew, was from Wattley, the marshal of the stables and head groomsman. Sir Gerald had introduced Thomas to him earlier.

Thomas poked his head out around Eclipse's

stall. There was the strange boy who'd stolen the apple yesterday! And angrily hoisting him up into the air was Marshal Wattley. It looked like the boy had been caught trying to feed the apple to Heartwind.

"Don't you have a brain in your skull?" Marshal Wattley snarled. "No one approaches the king's horse. God's truth, that horse will be the end of you, and I'll have to get me a new stable

boy. That's a dangerous animal." With that, Wattley tossed the boy onto the ground. As he left, he ordered, "Get back to mucking out stalls. And no more stunts."

Thomas came out of Eclipse's stall. The boy didn't look hurt. He was smiling as he stood up and brushed himself off. Thomas raised a hand. "Hello."

The stable boy grinned broadly at Thomas. "Hullo!" he said, and nodded, indicating the apple, still in his hand. "Heartwind wanted to take it. Dangerous animal! Pah. Old Wattley just doesn't know how to approach Heartwind, that's all. He's too frightened, and the horse knows it." Then the stable boy bit into the apple and happily chewed it himself. When he finished, he threw the core into a nearby bucket and held out his hand. "I'm Jon, the stable boy."

Thomas smiled and stretched out his hand. "I'm Thomas."

chapter 4

Jon was Thomas's first friend at the castle. If Marshal Wattley wasn't around, Jon would point out any new or interesting equipage on the horses of the visitors. And he continued to feed the king's warhorse treats—whenever he could get any.

One day Thomas was making his way to the stables along the inner wall of the castle ward when Jon blurred past. "C'mon! I'll race you to Heartwind's stall." Jon did not stop. "Bet I'll beat you there!"

"No you won't!" yelled Thomas.

They raced past the dovecote, which was

covered with white droppings the doves had made as they entered or left the many openings cut into its walls. The startled coos of the birds roosting inside drifted out as they sprinted by.

When they ducked behind the smithy, with its woodpile on one side and mound of cooling ashes on the other, Jon kicked up some ashes. They showered down on both of them. The blacksmith roared out the door and threw his arms up in disgust at the boys. Then Jon flew into the stables, past the piles of mucked-out manure and old bedding straw, past Bartholomew, and . . . *aiiii!* He fell across the threshold of Heartwind's stall.

The stall bars had been pulled open, and Thomas was right behind Jon. Together they slid through old straw and horse droppings and landed right at the foot of someone standing quietly in the stall.

Heartwind reared, snorted, and yanked his head up. He pranced in a tight circle, whinnying and shaking his head.

Jon and Thomas sprang to their feet and brushed themselves off. They tried not to laugh, for someone was there, consoling the horse.

"Shh. Shh . . . it's nothing. Just a couple of boys. Heartwind, shhhhhh."

Thomas stood silently next to Jon. He wasn't sure whether to look up or not. He kept his head down, expecting a sound cuffing, but he raised his eyes slightly. He could see the hem of a white kirtle and skirts of green and blue fabric hitched up slightly. Thomas followed Jon's lead and bowed when he heard Jon say, "Your Highness." Now he didn't dare raise his eyes!

Your Highness? Could this be the princess, or was it a visitor to the castle? Thomas knew there was a princess living at the castle. She was the king's only child, but he'd never laid eyes on her. She took her meals with the women of the castle and not in the great hall.

"Jon," said a female voice, "whatever are you doing?"

"We fell," Jon mumbled.

"I can see that," said the voice. The comment was followed by a suppressed laugh.

Maybe we won't get cuffed after all, thought Thomas. But he kept his shoulders hunched up and his head down, just in case.

Jon fumbled in his pocket for a moment. "I was bringing this to Heartwind," he said. Jon pulled a pear from his pocket. "It's a bit bruised. I got it from Dilley."

Dilley was one of the kitchen maids. The pear, Thomas could see, was more than a little bruised. It was flat on one side. Jon had probably landed on it.

"If you please, Princess Eleanor," said Jon, and he handed the pear to her.

It was the princess! Thomas raised his eyes a little more; he had to see her. She was wearing a green and blue gown with long sleeves. Her dark hair was caught up behind her. Oh! And he was standing so close to her! He gulped. Wouldn't his ma and da want to hear of this!

Then he looked down at his own ash-covered rough clothes. To make matters worse, bits of straw and horse dung hung off him. Maybe Ma and Da wouldn't want to hear about this. Thomas tried to brush some of the filth off without drawing attention to himself.

It didn't work. Princess Eleanor was staring at him. "Is this a new stable boy?"

"No, Your Highness," said Jon, elbowing Thomas in the side.

Thomas bowed again and introduced himself. "If I . . . if I may be of service, Your Highness. I am Thomas, page to Sir Gerald."

This time the princess did laugh out loud. "I am not sure what service you may do me at the moment, Thomas. Perhaps in the future, when you are more . . . more"—she struggled for a word—"more *refreshingly* attired. I do eat with my father's courtiers at times in the hall. If you ever attend at high table, you may do me a service at that time."

Then she smiled at Thomas and Jon and added, "Well, Jon, it seems you and I are of the same mind, for I have just given Heartwind a treat. Please don't tell Marshal Wattley! He thinks I spoil the horse, but I think our marshal is jealous because Heartwind can barely tolerate him. I can't help myself; he's a magnificent animal." She paused and added softly, "I don't get many free hours to visit."

Then she considered the two boys and the damaged pear. "There!" she said, taking a deep breath and settling her shoulders. "I have told you my *secretest* secret. All my ladies-in-waiting would be scandalized to know that sometimes what I desire most in the world is to slip away to visit my friends in the stables. Now"—she looked very seriously first at Jon and then at Thomas—"we are fellow conspirators and must henceforth always come to the aid of each other and any creature that needs our help. Agreed?"

Thomas could barely swallow. Were all princesses like this one? Somehow, he didn't think so. Thomas solemnly nodded. He saw Jon doing the same.

"I know," said the princess. "Let's give this pear to Bartholomew! Sweet donkey, he's been a friend of mine since I was a child, and Heartwind just had a treat." Then the princess strode out of the stall toward Bartholomew's pen.

Thomas and Jon closed up Heartwind's stall and timidly followed the princess, who had already stretched out her hand with the treat toward the donkey. "There, kind sir," she said, and stroked his gray muzzle as he ate it. "He used to pull my cart when I was a child."

Jon and Thomas kept silent as they stood alongside the princess and listened to Bartholomew chew. Finally, Princess Eleanor brushed off her hands and gathered herself together. She said, "Well, enough loitering for one day. I've work to attend to, what with all this scurrying about and preparing men to ride out to the border. I'm sure the two of you do as well. I meant to make only a short visit to Heartwind. However, I am happy to have discovered two champions in my quest to keep Heartwind from being so lonely." With that, she turned and left the stables.

Jon and Thomas bowed as the princess strode off across the inner ward. Then they looked at each other and smiled.

"Conspirators!" whispered Jon.

"Champions!" whispered Thomas.

Book II

A Blade from a Distant Land

chapter 5

Before Thomas could be a champion, he knew he needed to learn how to wield a sword and a shield, how to fight on horseback, and so many other things. All he'd really learned so far, besides how to be mannerly to visitors in the dining hall, was how to build a model battering ram. That had been a fun exercise on a particularly stormy day. But Thomas saw that more and more of the older boys were being sent away to the borderlands to perform really worthwhile tasks—boys who weren't even old enough to be knights yet. In fact, there were fewer and fewer squires in the castle, and many of the pages were starting to do some of the chores that had been done by older boys, like serving at the high table in the hall or accompanying the king's visitors on hunting trips and caring for the hunting falcons.

Yet it seemed to Thomas that he might never have a chance to do anything useful at all—until finally, one day, he was told to appear on the green before the castle to begin his sword training. The "swords" were only blunted pieces of wood with padded tips, but they were long and heavy like real two-handed fighting swords. Thomas knew this was just a first step—to get used to the weight and feel of a sword. What a surprise it was!

He could hardly lift the piece of wood. *They've weighted it with lead,* he thought. In addition, it was too long for Thomas's short arms. He could not lift it from the hilt end but had to grasp it farther up the shaft. Thomas grappled with it. Finally, leaning back a bit, he managed to raise the heavy tip from the ground and steady the whole thing against the front of his body. He had no idea how he was supposed to pick up a buckler as well. The small round shields were piled in a mound before the boys, and as Thomas struggled to bend down and get a buckler, his eyes rose to meet those of the bigger boys standing around the arms master. Several of them were trying not to laugh out loud. One tall blond boy named Edwin was shaking his head as if Thomas was a pitiful sight.

Thomas felt a tightness in his chest. Heat rushed to his cheeks, and he heard throbbing in his ears. He lowered his eyes. All his life he'd had to make up for his size. He knew he had more difficulty mastering some skills than others did, and he tried never to let that bother him. He thought it very unfair to be made fun of when he was doing his best!

The only ones not laughing were a couple of younger boys who were having the same problem. Even the arms master seemed to be biting the inside of his cheeks to keep from chortling. *What more do they want from me?* he wondered. *I'll show them!*

He grasped the training sword toward its middle and violently jerked upward on the heavy piece of wood to settle it across his shoulder, where he might be able to handle it more easily. Instead, it flew up and cracked him on his forehead.

Thomas staggered from the blow.

Edwin and the older boys burst out laughing.

"Master Thomas," said the instructor, "were that a real sword, you would have just saved me the futility of training you by splitting your head atwain."

Thomas nodded groggily as tears came to his eyes. His head *did* feel as if he'd split it in two. It hurt so much that he threw the training sword down, clutched his head, and stumbled from the field. "Stupid! Stupid! Stupid!" he muttered to himself as he staggered beyond the whoops of laughter.

One of the last things he heard was Edwin's haughty voice saying, "Well, it seems Sir Gerald's *little* pity case is trying to knock some sense into himself. I doubt it will work."

After which there followed more laughter, and then a barked command from the arms master. "All right, you younger page boys tuck the hilt as far up under your arm as you can!"

Later, Sir Gerald called Thomas in to speak with him. "The arms master has spoken with me about difficulties in your training," he said.

"Yes," said Thomas. "I . . ." He swallowed hard, not wanting to admit how foolish he'd been. He'd slunk away like a dog with its tail between its legs; now he'd never be able to go back without getting laughed at again. The other boys probably thought he'd been pouting all day. What if it meant he'd have to leave? He couldn't become a knight, or a squire, or even a champion of any sort, without knowing how to handle a sword! He continued, "I . . . I had a problem with the practice swords."

"Hmm," said Sir Gerald, pushing back Thomas's hair to see all of the large, ugly bruise on the boy's forehead. "I can see that. Did you have this tended to?"

"Yes. Cook put a poultice on it."

"I understand you were mocked by the others?"

Thomas looked down at the floor. He nodded.

"And you left the practice field?"

Again Thomas nodded. "Yes."

Sir Gerald paused thoughtfully and then told the boy, "It is good to have pride. But what weak knights we would make if, whenever invaders scoffed us, we threw our arms down and walked

51

away." He let Thomas think about that for a time while he paced the room. He returned to stand before the boy. "And you let anger get in the way of your purpose. Who has lost the most thereby?"

Thomas's voice caught in his throat. He'd disappointed Sir Gerald. And certainly his father would be disappointed in him if he heard of this. *Da!* Thomas groaned inwardly. His da, who'd wanted to be a knight himself . . .

For as far back as he could remember, Thomas had wanted to go on adventurous quests so he could come home and tell his father stories about the wondrous things of the world—things his father had never gotten to see—things Thomas knew were out there. He could not imagine going home and telling Da he'd failed! If he got sent away in shame, he wouldn't be able to go back home—not like that. Thomas took a wavery deep breath. Sir Gerald was right, and now he wanted to hear it from Thomas. *Who has lost the most by this foolish behavior?* "I . . . I have," he answered.

"No!" shouted the knight.

Thomas jerked up his head to stare wide-eyed at him.

"It is the kingdom that loses. We stand to lose much if we are not prepared—if we do not have trained pages and skillful squires who will become knights to protect our homes and our families. It is only by the thinnest thread that we make our homes in relative peace with our neighbors. To do this takes skill in all areas of training, and wisdom to know and do one's duty despite laughter or pain. *Here,* you train for the kingdom, not for yourself! Never forget that."

Thomas's mouth dropped open. He'd never thought about the gravity of the duties a member of the King's Company took on. He *had* to be given another chance. How could he live with himself if he failed his kingdom, too? "Please—"

Sir Gerald interrupted him by laying a hand on the boy's shoulder. In a kinder tone he said, "You are young yet. These are lessons that need to be learned. Remember this—anger has its purpose, but never let it keep you from doing what you must."

Thomas gulped and nodded. He started to say how sorry he was. Sir Gerald waved him away but then stopped him as he turned to leave. The knight added, "Also, I've talked to some of the training masters. We will be increasing your weapons training, and you will be starting dance and music along with religious studies soon. I would not have them keep you too long with the youngest of the pages."

"Da-a-ance?" Thomas squeaked, slowly coming around to face the knight. His face was pale.

"Dance," said Sir Gerald, looking at Thomas with a smile. "A squire or a knight must be ready for any eventuality. We pride ourselves on being well versed in all the arts, social as well as military." Then Sir Gerald laughed and clapped Thomas heartily on the shoulder. "Do not fear, Thomas. I am sure you'll be light on your feet and do quite well."

The next day, Thomas returned to sword practice. He could see the others peeking at his forehead. Edwin seemed particularly pleased by the sight of Thomas's injury.

Thomas tried not to think of their stares or to hear the low twitters and chuckles as he slowly, over the weeks that followed, became used to the ungainly training weapons. It was difficult—especially when the larger boys ridiculed him. He still got angry, but he never let it distract him from his training again.

Besides, the other boys soon learned there were times when being small was to Thomas's advantage. He was a much quicker and more difficult target to hit when practicing with padded staffs. In addition, he was the best at ducking out of the way of the whirling quintain when stabbing the dummy with a lance.

The other boys were hit repeatedly by the dummy's sand-stuffed arms and knocked off the wooden "horse" that was pushed at the quintain. But not Thomas. Thomas could jab and then duck low enough along the back of the wooden sawhorse that he avoided the dummy's arms. This made Edwin and some of the larger boys cast dirty looks at Thomas when they limped from the field. Thomas *was* light on his feet.

And Sir Gerald was right—he was light on his feet during dance lessons with Princess Eleanor's ladies-in-waiting as well. Thomas had hoped to see the princess during these lessons, but she

seemed so busy that there were only a few moments when he was able to glimpse her from afar.

Nevertheless, Thomas attended to all his studies as a page and served Sir Gerald faithfully and well. Until one day, upon a return visit by Sir Gerald to the castle, when Thomas was asked to wait upon his knight in the chapel.

chapter 6

Thomas found Sir Gerald in the small chapel off the great hall. He was on his knees, praying. At his side lay a small scabbard and a shield, not Sir Gerald's own magnificent sword and shield. Thomas studied a faded painting in the chapel as Sir Gerald prayed. It depicted a dragon terrorizing a village, and reminded Thomas of Da's many stories of knights and dragons. He was suddenly homesick.

He'd been at the castle for some months now and had managed to make it home a few times. Still, he often wished he could visit more. *Soon,* he thought.

Sir Gerald rose and approached him. "Thomas," he said, "I have had good reports from your instructors. You are an apt pupil, even managing to ride one of the castle ponies with some agility. And the ladies tell me that your dancing is above adequate."

Thomas blushed.

"Also," continued the knight, "though I was in a hurry to get here, I did stop to share a meal with your father on my way."

"How is he? And the family, sir?"

"They are well. The new baby is healthy and hungry all the time. Your little sister Isabel is very vocal. She has apparently learned a good many new words. And Peter seems to have acquired another layer of dirt, which he was happy to share with me."

Thomas smiled, despite a twist of pain in his stomach. He realized how much he missed them all. However, he forced himself to turn his attention back to Sir Gerald, who was studying Thomas thoughtfully. It was obvious the knight had more about which he wished to speak.

Finally, Sir Gerald cleared his throat and said,

"You've got more than thirteen years now. This is a little young, but it's not unheard of for a squire to be thirteen, provided his studies have been successful."

Thomas jerked upright. *A squire?* His eyes grew wide as he listened to Sir Gerald.

"I am, perhaps, rushing things along a bit," the knight said. "You have not had the benefit of years of study, as most pages have. However, I have faith in your ability to learn quickly. These are dire times, and mayhap the days ahead will grow even darker before we see some relief. I have need of a new squire to accompany me, to aid in dressing Eclipse and me for battle, to see to the replenishing and repair of my weapons, to care for Eclipse in the field, and to run errands as I require them. The other boys I have trained have long since been stationed on our borders, for the king is employing every able hand he can. Therefore, I would have you now take your place by my side. Do you understand what I am saying?"

Thomas nodded. *A squire!* He could hardly wait to tell his family.

Sir Gerald was not finished. He added, "These

are not easy tasks and require fortitude, and loy-
alty to me, your knight."

"I—I understand."

"Good. Then I have for you some things you
will need." The knight picked up the scabbard and
shield. "As my squire, you have earned the right to
carry my coat of arms." He handed Thomas the
small shield, upon which was blazoned a field of
blue, quartered. In one quarter was a lion ram-
pant, which was the symbol of the king. In another was Sir Gerald's House of Wellsford arms, a

red rose above a silver sword. In the top two quarters were a burning castle and two fleurs-de-lis representing the families of the king. "It may be some time yet before you will need a full-sized shield."

Thomas ran his fingers lightly over the shield. He didn't care that it was small, like the castle's practice bucklers, and he was about to say so when Sir Gerald had in his hands an even more wonderful gift. It was the small scabbard, inlaid with intertwining vines rising from a pool and topped by starflowers. In the morning light from the chapel's window, the hilt glinted with silver.

Thomas pulled the sword from its scabbard. It was short, but a perfect fit for him. The two sides of the blade were thin and sharp, and the tip curved a bit. Around the hilt was a knotted cord of silver, but the most unusual part of the sword was the hilt itself. It was carved and old, and looked to be made of ivory. Thomas could make out a lake and clouds in the carvings, and—he wasn't sure— something else that looked like a cave or tunnel entrance. It was all so mysterious and beautiful. He opened his mouth, but nothing came out.

Sir Gerald smiled down at the boy. "There's an interesting story about the blade," he pointed out. "I think it's important that you know it." The knight sat down upon a bench. "I'm not sure what to make of it myself. You see, the iron of this sword was forged across the eastern ocean and, through various routes, made its way to our land. But the sword had no hilt. Apparently, a sword-smith kept it displayed above his wares but would not sell the blade to any who asked about it. Always his response was that one day the blade would be given a hilt of great antiquity, and then he would know what to do with the sword.

"One morning this swordsmith went to the wharves to purchase a fish for a special dinner. When the cook sliced into the fish—lo and behold!—he found a large ivory tooth. It was very old, and none could tell from what sort of creature the tooth came. But upon seeing it, the smith knew that an ivory hilt must be carved from the tooth for the blade that hung in his shop. This he did, he said, in a dreamlike daze. When he finished carving, he joined the hilt to the blade with a rope of silver. As he worked, he heard a phrase repeated in his head: *not made for taking, but for giving.* So he never sold or bartered the finished sword. He had it for many years.

"Well, a fortnight ago I was traveling through a village when I happened to pass the swordsmith's shop. I was quite surprised when the fellow ran out into the road and gripped me by the arm, saying I was just the person he'd been waiting for. And then he gave me this sword! I wanted to give him something in return, for as you can see, it is exquisite. He would not hear of it. It was a gift, he said. He was very emphatic about that—repeating that it was not meant for taking, but for giving. He finished by saying that I would know the brave heart whose hand it would fit."

Thomas gulped. He asked, "Do you think I have a brave heart?"

Sir Gerald smiled again. "I'm certain you do. See, it fits your hand well! At any rate," he added, scratching his beard, "I have spent the morning praying upon it, and I feel the sword was meant for you. It was given to me, and now I give it to you. Treat it with great care. The swordsmith called the blade Starfast. Do you like that name? You can change it if you wish."

"No . . . I mean, yes. Yes! I like that name. And no, I don't want to change it," spluttered Thomas. "And I *do* promise to care for it. Do you think the hilt's made from a whale's tooth?" He'd heard of those beasts of the water, though he'd never seen one.

The knight shrugged. "I don't know. Perhaps it is made of the stuff of stars. But," he said, "I do know that I have other duties to attend to today. As do you. We leave tonight, and Marshal Wattley must be told. Well, Squire Thomas—for so I hereby dub thee—keep safe your new blade, Starfast. It is short, but sharp and finely made, with a hilt carved from the tooth of an ancient being. May it ever serve our king, and thee, and me."

Thus did Thomas become a squire.

Squire Thomas had no time to return home to see his family. He barely had time to strap on his sword and scurry to the stables to inform Marshal Wattley that all must be prepared for Sir Gerald to leave that evening.

He did take a few moments to find Jon and tell him the news.

When Thomas pulled Starfast from its scabbard,

Jon's eyes grew large, and he whistled. "It's the most beautiful thing I've ever seen," Jon said, "except for Heartwind, of course." Then he quickly added, "Or the princess."

Thomas nodded.

"And the hilt is carved from a tooth?"

"An *ancient* tooth," Thomas said. "Maybe a whale's—"

"Or a dragon's!" Jon exclaimed.

Thomas caught his breath. He hadn't thought of that.

Jon touched Starfast gingerly. "It's the blade of a champion," he said. "And now you're going off to the borderlands with Sir Gerald. It's just like the princess said, conspirators and *champions*."

When they left that night, Sir Gerald and Eclipse led the way. Despite proudly wearing Starfast, Thomas followed behind on a cart with the supplies.

They visited many of the camps in the North Country, delivering supplies. Sir Gerald also met with other knights, repositioned men along the front, and carried out the king's instructions.

When he found time from his chores, Thomas listened to other squires he met in the North Country. He heard their hair-raising tales of battles and bloodshed. Secretly, he was glad that he and Sir Gerald had not yet encountered any troops from across the border. In fact, he would have been happy to return to the castle without having seen a battle.

However, that was not to be. Thomas's first skirmish as Sir Gerald's squire took place high in the mountains. The knights were fighting on foot in a deep pass. The ground was rocky and uneven, so the horses were held on a plateau below the pass. Thomas spent the whole of the battle holding on to Eclipse's reins and soothing the horse. The clashing and clanking sounds of steel, drifting down to him from above, frightened Thomas, too. Mingled with those sounds were the cries of men. He strained to hear individual voices. What if Sir Gerald was injured?

Around him other squires waited, white-knuckled, gripping the reins of other warhorses. And Thomas could hear nervous whispers of "Steady! Steady!" He wondered if these words of encouragement were for the horses or for the squires themselves.

Suddenly there was movement at the edge of the group. A runner had come from the battle, bearing a shield. Then a tall, thin boy quietly donned a mail shirt, picked up the shield carried from the battlefield, and handed the reins of his knight's warhorse to another. Thomas knew what was happening; if a knight should fall, his squire would enter the battle in his stead. Thomas watched the boy leave, wondering if he would see him again.

Thomas thought of Da's stories of knights and quests. How childish they seemed compared to the tortured screams he heard coming from the nearby battle. Here a real fight was raging and real people were getting hurt. He wasn't so sure he was ready to be a champion.

Thomas's hand strayed to Starfast, belted tightly at his side. He looked at Eclipse. The horse trusted him. But if called to do his duty, he'd do the same as the boy who had just left. He'd hand Eclipse's reins over to a stranger. Then he'd march into the fray, Starfast in hand. That thought made his insides quiver.

Fortunately, Sir Gerald was skilled in the fighting arts whether on horseback or on foot. After this and other battles, Thomas tended to Sir Gerald's cuts and bruises and made sure to secure replacements for any lost or broken maces or lances. And once, on a foggy morning when a small company of the king's men was surprised by a group of northern invaders, Thomas darted—without thinking—through the battlefield to retrieve a dropped battle-ax for Sir Gerald.

At the time, he was roundly chastised and told to *get back!* However, later, the knight and Thomas's fellow squires praised his bravery.

It was quite a bit later—when he'd had time to think about what he'd done—that Thomas's legs began to wobble uncontrollably.

chapter 7

After many months Sir Gerald
and Thomas returned home. The knight, with
other knights, rode ahead. Thomas, with other
squires, followed the knights on foot. Word had
come from the castle of a special gathering. A new
group of squires was to be knighted in response to
the call for more men. This announcement caused
a great deal of gossip among the boys. It was well
known that if a squire showed great courage, the
king could knight him, even if he hadn't attained
eighteen years or wasn't old enough to join a
guild. In an emergency, a knight could even ele-
vate his own squire to knighthood.

Thomas was sure the tall, thin boy who'd gone so bravely into battle after his knight had fallen would be among the new knights. The boy had been wounded but had lived to tell of the battle.

And what about himself? Hadn't he also proven his courage? Several of the other squires seemed to think so. He'd scooted around charging horses and ducked under swinging swords to retrieve Sir Gerald's battle-ax. At the time Thomas hadn't thought it was so brave. He'd simply reacted, much as he'd done when play-fighting and darting out of the way of the quintain's swinging arms during his training. Now he wondered . . . might he possibly be on the lists of the king? After all, Sir Gerald had been called back as well.

At the hushed gathering, Thomas was squashed between Sir Gerald, several other knights, and many squires. They were all so much taller than Thomas that he could only see the king or Princess Eleanor at the front of the chamber when a gap happened to open up in the crowd.

All of the older squires expected to take the oath of fealty this day, and some of the younger

ones hoped for it. Thomas carefully nurtured his own small hope that Sir Gerald had told the king of his courageous deed on the battlefield. Perhaps . . .

He tried to calm his racing heart by peeking at the princess whenever he got the chance. Her smile was kindly, as he had remembered it.

It did not surprise him that she hovered over the elderly king, assisting him with his duties. Today, Thomas thought she looked like the queen she would one day be. The circlet of jewels she wore above her braided hair shone like stars. *Like stars in a dark sky,* Thomas thought as he awaited the command of his liege. He wanted so much to serve his king—and the princess.

Today Thomas stood hopefully awaiting his part in the ritual. He was prepared. Last night he had taken the precaution of praying and meditating upon the duties of a knight. This morning he had bathed and fasted.

He gripped the hilt of Starfast in its scabbard at his waist. Oh, to be knighted by his king with his own sword!

Now the restless crowd hushed as each tall

squire around him was called forth one at a time. Each one knelt, presented his sword to the king, and was dubbed a knight. Thomas waited for his name to be called.

He waited in the warmth of the sunlight soaking in through the stained-glass window. He waited, repeating the words of the oath to himself: . . . *to the end of my days.* He knew the words by heart; every boy in training at the castle did. Thomas must have repeated them thousands of times while playing, and in his dreams.

He was still waiting as the king and princess rose. Bowing from the waist, Thomas caught a glimpse of them leaving. The arms master and a line of new knights followed them out. Then he saw, without anger or even surprise, that in addition to the brave squire Thomas had seen at his first battle, Edwin was among the newly knighted. Edwin, who had annoyed him so much during his training, shot him a nasty smile.

It was in that instant that Thomas understood something very important: no matter how hardworking he was, or how bravely he'd rendered service in a battle, he might *never* be good enough.

When the royal family had left the hall, Thomas straightened, and Sir Gerald squeezed his shoulder for a long moment. "You're still young, Thomas. You've not got but fourteen years," he said kindly.

"Don't worry, I'll be fine. I've got . . . more training to do, that's all."

Sir Gerald nodded and followed the crowd out.

Finally—thankfully—Thomas was alone in the darkening room.

chapter 8

Thomas remained at the castle for some weeks after the day of the ceremony. He attended to more studies Sir Gerald arranged for him, and he traveled with his knight whenever Sir Gerald left the castle. They rarely spoke of that afternoon in the great hall.

One day Sir Gerald left to oversee some reinforcing of his own great hall in Wellsford, and Thomas was not needed to ride out with him. A few days later, Thomas decided to visit his family. He strapped on Starfast and took a shortcut through the castle keep. As he passed one of the rarely used older corridors, Thomas thought he heard someone muttering. He unsheathed his sword and looked around.

In a gloom-fisted corner a figure slumped on a bench in an alcove. Cautiously Thomas approached. The person seemed to be speaking aloud, but Thomas did not see anyone else about. He came closer. It was the king! To whom was he speaking? Was he ill? Thomas put away his sword. He approached and bowed.

The king had a scrap of parchment in one hand, and the other hand was over his eyes. He mumbled, "Where are the champions of old? Where are the Galahads, the Sir Kays, of history? Oh, we have too few, too few knights now! In this dark time, where are the pure of heart when I need them?"

Thomas cleared his throat.

"What! Who . . ." The king dropped his hand and spied Thomas.

"Your Majesty, it is I, Thomas, squire to Sir Gerald." Thomas approached and bowed again. Then, at the king's feet, he knelt. "If you would have me, I will pledge my heart until the end of my days."

"Has it come to this?" the king whispered. He leaned forward. "Do only such small ones remain to serve?"

"My lord, it is true that I am not big," said Thomas, "but my heart is pure. I have, with all my love, served Sir Gerald. Now I would beg to serve my king and kingdom at this hour of need."

"Humph!" the king grunted, appraising Thomas. "You speak well, and gallantly. I've no doubt that your heart is pure. Even so, had I twenty knights as stout as Galahad, or Gerald, it would not be enough. So many of my men have gone to the border, or are seeing to the defenses of their own halls, that I've none here at home when . . ." He waved the parchment in the air and then looked away. After a long moment, he shuddered and continued, "When a slumbering vileness has reawakened. I've just had word that the dragon Bridgoltha has abducted the Princess Eleanor."

Thomas gasped. He knew the tales of Bridgoltha, the queen of the dragons. No one had seen the great she-dragon in years, and most people thought she'd died long ago on Barren Isle, the ancestral home of the dragons.

The dragon's name was rarely spoken aloud. There were reports that whole fields of wheat shriveled when she passed overhead, and that chickens who saw her stopped laying eggs. Thomas recalled the painting in the chapel—the scene of villagers fleeing in the shadow of a ferocious dragon. He wasn't sure if these old tales were true, but the thought that she still lived filled him with dread. He felt a sickening weakness seep into his bones.

Yet Thomas lowered his head, took a deep breath, and said, "My liege, I am but one, and perhaps . . . not stout. Still, I am one who has lived awaiting a great quest to serve my king."

The king sighed. "What do quests matter? The queen has been dead many years, and my only child abducted! I foolishly sent her to the western shores thinking to have her rally our friends from that region. Now . . ." The king threw his hands up in the air and the parchment floated down.

"I've no heir but Eleanor. And I've only a few

seasoned knights and some young boys, who may not return; so many are dying on the northern borders. What does any of it matter anymore?" he muttered, leaning back and waving a hand. "Bridgoltha has taken my Eleanor. Without her . . ." The king shrugged. He closed his eyes and said, "I am an old, old man." Then he seemed to sleep.

Thomas knelt and waited. He waited while dust motes danced through a single shaft of afternoon light that pierced the long corridor from a nearby arrow loop. He waited while the distant sounds of the castle came and went in the galleries around them. He waited while evening crept up and deepened the dark of the quiet corner.

Finally, the king shook himself and sat up. "Hmm? Are you still here?" Then, as though thinking aloud, he added, "Surely you are Gerald of Wellsford's page, not his squire?"

"I am his squire, my liege," answered Thomas.

"His squire? Are you the one who risked his life with Sir Gerald in battle?"

"I am," said Thomas, raising his eyes.

"Sir Gerald says you are quick and excelled at

avoiding the quintain's arms," said the king. "And I have had good reports of your studies, and your refusal to give in to defeat when others laughed at your stature."

"My mother has oft remarked upon my stubbornness, Sire."

At this, the king chuckled and then leaned forward as if to inspect Thomas. He placed his hand on Thomas's head. It was some long minutes before the king removed his hand and murmured, "So young . . . Oh! To be this young again, and full of hope."

Then the king roused himself and said in a more stately tone, "Squire Thomas."

Thomas raised his head fully to look upon his king. He was stiff from having knelt this whole time.

"Present your blade."

Thomas's hands shook as he pulled forth Starfast and held it aloft.

The king smiled—sad and quick—as he surveyed Thomas's blade, barely longer than a dagger. Still, he grasped the delicate sword and asked Thomas, "By what name do you call your blade?"

"Starfast, Your Majesty."

The king was pleased. "That is a fine name. One can always depend upon the stars, held fast to the sky." He turned the blade over in his hands, examining it. "Ah! An eastern blade. Greek, perhaps. Short, but elegant and finely made—a resilient blade, young man. And an interesting hilt, I see. It seems quite old. May it serve our kingdom well in the days to come."

Holding Starfast above Thomas's bowed head, the king intoned the opening lines of the oath of fealty.

> "This day, for king and country,
> do you, Thomas, pledge your heart
> to the right service of your liege,
> to the end of your days?"

And Thomas replied,

> "I, Thomas, do pledge
> my heart in right service
> to my liege and my country,
> to the end of my days."

The king lowered Starfast, gently touching first his new knight's right shoulder and then his left. "By the honorable blade Starfast, I, your king, command you to rise. Well met this day, Sir Thomas, Knight of the Realm."

chapter 9

Sir Thomas packed his few belongings. As the king had advised, he went to the stables to see if there was a pony that might serve as his mount.

Jon hooted and clapped Thomas on the back when he presented himself as *Sir* Thomas, a Knight of the Realm! He demanded to hear the story of Thomas's knighting several times and shook his head at the mention of Bridgoltha.

"I can't believe she lives," he said. "My da always said Bridgoltha would get us if we misbehaved. It used to scare the little ones into behaving. Not me, of course. Now the dragon queen's got our princess."

Jon waved his fist in the air. "I can hardly stomach it! Why, I'd go with you if I could, but Old Wattley's down with a bilious gut, and I am"—he bowed—"now an official *assistant under-groomsman*. I've got Heartwind to care for while the old fellow's taken to his bed. Don't tell him that I'm still conspiring to sneak treats to the horse, though."

Thomas hugged his friend. "Congratulations, new . . . um, assistant under-groomsman. . . ."

"Aye." Jon scratched his head. "I think that's what he called the position."

"Whatever you are, you're still a conspirator," Thomas added.

"And you"—Jon punched Thomas on the arm—"you are off to be a champion for our princess!" Then, suddenly, Jon backed away and bowed. "Sir Thomas," he said with a flourish.

Thomas blushed. He cleared his throat and said, "There are no ponies, are there, Jon?"

Jon rose. "I'm afraid not. The only horse in the stables is Heartwind. Sir Gerald took Eclipse and the two new ponies when he left."

Thomas nodded. No one other than the king rode Heartwind. Moreover, he knew he wouldn't have been able to mount him anyway. The best he'd been able to do in his training was to get astride one of the smaller ponies.

Well, it was a knight's lot to be tested. *I suppose I must walk to Barren Isle,* he told himself.

Then he spied Bartholomew. The cart donkey would be a good fit; he wouldn't need a helping hand to get atop the short, sturdy animal. "Could I have Bartholomew?"

"If you wish it!" spluttered Jon, trying to keep

from laughing. "But you know we've only the cart yoke for the donkey. There's no other equipage his size."

"A rope lead will do, and a blanket to protect his back," said Thomas. "There's no armor to fit me, so his back will not need extra padding."

That evening, Thomas and Bartholomew traveled as far as Thomas's home, where the two supped late. Some of Thomas's brothers and sisters were still awake and excited to see the new knight—their brother!—as well as Bartholomew. They hugged the uncomplaining donkey, tugged at his coarse short mane, and innocently poked him as they took turns climbing up and stroking him. Thomas also, for the first time, let them touch Starfast's hilt. They had seen the sword on previous visits, but this time Thomas let them touch the intricate carvings. That satisfied their curiosity for a while. Later, they crowded around asking one question after another.

"How come you don't have a *real* horse?" asked Albert, smirking.

Before Thomas could answer, Isabel piped up,

"I've got my real horse, Thomas, out of real wood. We could share him."

"You and your toy horse! It's so old and beat-up, you can hardly tell it's a horse anymore," Thomas teased her with a smile. However, he *was* pleased that at three years, Isabel had finally learned to share. "And I thank you for the offer," he added.

"What good is a toy wooden horse?" snapped Albert.

Thomas felt a tug on his sleeve. It was Peter.

"Where's your chain mail?" he asked. "Knights got chain mail or armor."

"He's no knight! Look at him," said Albert. "Who'd make him a knight?"

"Me!" shouted Isabel. "And Thomas said I should share. My horse is good for lots of things, so there," she added, sticking her tongue out at Albert.

"Don't stick your tongue out," said Thomas, tapping Isabel lightly on the top of her head. "It's rude."

"Hush!" said Ma, suddenly sweeping into the cottage and shooing several of the children off

Thomas's lap and toward the sleeping loft. "If Thomas says he was knighted today, then he *was* knighted. That's the top and the bottom of it! Now off to bed with you, and quit pestering your brother. *Sir* Thomas has a long day ahead of him tomorrow."

That night, Thomas told his parents of his quest to Barren Isle to rescue Princess Eleanor from the dragon queen, Bridgoltha. His mother's face turned ashen. "Can't your quest be a bit closer to home?" she squeaked, grabbing at his hands and holding them tight.

"Ma, I *must* go. The king is old, and it will not be long before we need the princess to be queen. The king is afraid everything he's worked for will fall to ruin if there is no heir. Who would protect the borders? War could come to us here at home. I'm the only one who can go; all of the other knights are away."

Thomas's father cleared his throat. "Barren Isle—it's a dangerous first quest," he said. "But you're a knight! The king has entrusted you with this. I've no doubt you'll succeed."

Thomas slipped his hands from his mother's grasp and rubbed them nervously on his knees. He turned to his father. "Yes, I'm a knight. But I . . . I have doubts, Da."

"Thomas, it's fine to have doubts. Just don't let 'em eat you up," his father said. "I've heard tales from the castle that you've been every bit as good a squire as others. And brave, to boot! Now you'll be every bit as good a knight as the king's other knights. Better, even!" He slapped Thomas on the thigh and continued, "As your father, I know something you may not know."

"What?" asked Thomas.

"You've no idea what talents lie within you. Me? I'm only a rough tradesman; my talent is in my hands." Thomas's father looked for a moment at his large, scarred hands. "But you . . . your talents are here." He laid a hand on his son's chest and held it there a moment. "They are deep within you. One day, I've no doubt, you'll draw upon those natural talents, and they will not fail you. Mark my words, son. Other things may fall away, but what you find within . . . *that* you can always rely upon."

Suddenly shy, his father dropped his hand and nodded. He rose and lumbered out the door toward his workshop. His mother put a hanky to her nose and waved Thomas off to bed.

In the morning, Thomas found a pouch packed and waiting for him. His mother had stayed awake all night baking and preparing for his journey. She had stuffed a bag with breads, hard cheese, and a wax-covered honey cake that would keep for many days.

After breakfast, with his family gathered around, his father presented him with a wrapped bundle. Thomas opened it. Inside was a buff-colored leather jerkin with finely worked details and three intricately crafted silver clasps to tighten the vest around him. The delicacy of the designs Da had pressed into the leather took Thomas's breath away. He looked at his tired father, unable to find the words to thank him.

His father said, "I started it soon after you became Sir Gerald's squire. A gift for the day my son would become a knight, because I never doubted you. Look!" His father took it and held it open. "It's padded with the dried bark of a cork tree, which I bought at the fair. They say the stuff comes all the way from across the sea. It will keep you dry and warm and offer some protection from harm."

He touched his son's shoulder. "Take care with it, for this leather and the silver of the clasps are worth much. And there's this, which I fashioned last night." He held out a set of reins and a small metal bit for Bartholomew. "I didn't have time to make more."

Thomas took them, studying the patterned embossing on the leather of the reins. He raised his eyes. "They're beautiful, Da."

"Mayhap they will help in your quest and bring you home all the sooner."

Thomas put on his leather jerkin. Then he covered the calmly waiting Bartholomew with his blanket and belted it tight. He hung his pouch from the wide belt around Bartholomew, and put the new bit and reins on the donkey. They fit perfectly.

Now Thomas had Starfast and his shield from Sir Gerald, Bartholomew from the king's stables, his vest and leather reins from his father, and a pouch of provisions from his mother. He was ready to venture forth.

Isabel tugged at the pouch hanging from Bartholomew. Thomas grabbed her and hugged her. Then he swung her through the air until she giggled. Lastly, he kissed his parents good-bye. For a goodly way down the lane, Sir Thomas could see his family waving as he rode out upon a quest for his king.

Book III

Toward an Ancient Evil

chapter 10

Thomas had never traveled to Barren Isle before. Indeed, very few had done so and lived to tell the tale. He only knew that it must be west and a bit north along the dark coast of the sea, for many of the old tales told of the people of this region battering back the attacks of dragons. It was said the dragons had taken their treasure and retreated to caves that were burrowed into the two jagged peaks on that desolate island.

The going was steady but slow, as Bartholomew stopped often to munch grasses that grew upon the increasingly rolling hills. Villages grew fewer and farther apart as they traveled.

Yet from every holding, cottagers would wander out to speak with the young traveler and smile when he introduced himself as a Knight of the Realm. In addition, Bartholomew got hugs and bits of turnips from the children they met. In some places, adults snickered behind their hands at such an unlikely knight questing to the island of the dragons. Often, Thomas heard people whisper, "Imagine that!" or saw them shake their heads as though bewildered.

The news of the journey spread faster than Sir Thomas could travel on Bartholomew. Many times he was awaited and welcomed to share meals and shelter—no matter how humble—with families along the way. The young knight was glad of this, for it made his provisions last longer. In exchange, he regaled his listeners with talk of life in the castle, of battles, and of Isabel and the rest of his family.

Some folk of this hill country told him tales as well, especially as the countryside grew steeper and wilder. These stories were often rumors of great wealth in the dragon's lair. However, the stories that struck Thomas the most were those told by solemn folk of a dark pool of water along the coast. Split off from the cleansing waters of the sea, this stagnant swamp had given birth to a monster. Any who wished to journey to Barren Isle had to first make it past the many-headed beast of the lake.

All who whispered of it said the monster devoured passersby by catching them in its long tentacles and tearing them to pieces with its several mouths. It was a cursed lake that had cast a shadow upon the lands nearby. It was foretold that the only way anyone could survive its watery grasp, and defeat the beast of the lake, would be to return to the beast what was taken from it. Since no one—they all agreed—knew what that was, the land about the lake was doomed to be a forbidding place.

Thomas had worried about coming face to face with the dragon who had taken the princess; now it seemed there was another beast to deal with. He wondered if he might be able to sneak past it if he had to venture near the lake. He was small and good at being quiet. His quest was to rescue the princess, not kill a monster. Thomas did not want to draw down the creature's wrath if he could avoid it. He shivered. After all, there would be the dragon to confront, and one such task would be plenty.

Sometimes a spark of anger would flare within him, for it seemed to Thomas that certain people smirked as they warned him of the beast, of its devouring heads and its many small mouths all biting and chewing. He wasn't sure if they were trying to shake his resolve or make fun of him. Then he would remember his training and the lessons of Sir Gerald. He would do what he had come to do and not let anger, or fear, rule him.

Still, in the dark of the night, he wished he could simply turn around and hurry home. He questioned the strength of his hand and his heart. Was Da right? Was he really good enough to be a knight? When he'd been brave on the battlefield with Sir Gerald, he'd acted without thinking. He'd simply seen what needed to be done and had done it. But this was different. This was more like the squire who'd quietly—knowingly—walked into battle to do his best. That was a deliberate kind of bravery. Did he possess *that* kind of bravery?

Would he be able to draw upon those talents Da spoke of—and did he really have any talent at all?

Thomas pushed back his doubts; he did not have time to dwell upon them now. His road led toward the coast and Barren Isle—regardless of whatever he might meet along the way. In the end he was more determined than ever to do what he must, and he pushed Bartholomew to quicken his pace.

Several days later, Thomas and Bartholomew found themselves welcomed at a small cottage by an elderly widow who fed them quite well. Beyond her home the road narrowed to a faint trail, and the wayfarers passed a whole afternoon without coming upon another village, or even a small farm holding. It wasn't until early evening that the two happened upon a deserted cottage. There was something so sad about the place that Thomas did not want to sleep within it. He and Bartholomew settled in the lee of the crumbling walls, and Thomas lit a cooking fire.

Suddenly Bartholomew raised his head, swiveled his ears back, and turned toward a nearby hill.

"What is it?" Thomas asked as Bartholomew brayed loudly and struggled to rise.

Quickly Thomas studied the hilly countryside. Passing in the distance was a small group of men on foot. In the dusk Thomas could just make out that some carried raised staffs. He saw only a single rider on a horse. It was an immense silver-gray stallion. Then the last rays of the setting sun raked downward and lit a blue flag in the midst of the group.

"The king's banner!" cried Thomas, running back to Bartholomew. "We must hurry!" He knew the king wouldn't have left the castle unless there was the gravest need. Perhaps it was further news of the princess? Or a disaster near one of the borders? As quickly as he could, Thomas doused the campfire, repacked their bags, retrieved Bartholomew's blanket and belt, grabbed the reins from the broken back of the cottage door, and mounted up.

Then Bartholomew picked his way over the hill, carefully and very slowly.

They were too late. The king and his men had already passed, and in the deepening twilight

Thomas could not see them ahead on the path. He patted Bartholomew on the neck. "That's all right," he said, swallowing his disappointment. "We're sure to catch up sooner or later."

For a long time they plodded after the king. They followed the trail until the deep night blinded them to the way, and they stopped to give in to sleep.

chapter 11

In the morning Thomas saw that the countryside was much wilder. Brambles and curtains of vines grew up into stunted trees. Moss-covered boulders overhung dark openings into the earth. There was no wind.

However, Thomas could see the path the king and his men had taken—vines had been slashed to clear the way. Bartholomew needed some coaxing to follow, for an ill feeling was settling upon them. They rode along, only stopping briefly when there was a wisp of green Bartholomew could nibble.

Sir Thomas stayed mounted for most of the

morning. He hung his head in the still air and nodded sleepily on Bartholomew's back, trusting the sure-footed donkey. Except for the thud of Bartholomew's hooves, and occasionally some gentle encouragement by Thomas, the two passed most of the way in silence.

Toward midday Thomas was roused—not by noise or wind or cold, but by a stink so vile he suddenly stiffened, sitting alert on Bartholomew's back. His eyes watered as he swiveled to look about, trying to find the source of the stench. Bartholomew jerked to a stop and brayed piteously. *Haw-aw-aw!*

Sir Thomas leapt off Bartholomew and drew Starfast. He peered into the tangles of brush on either side of the path. They had been going downhill for some time, and the undergrowth had grown denser as they descended from the higher forests. Now the path had changed from rocky to mushy. Just ahead, the path left by the king and his men made a sharp turn past tall, willowy grasses. Thomas could not see around the bend.

The air felt different, too. It was wetter

and clung with a heaviness that made it difficult to breathe. The smell didn't help. Thomas pulled the tail of his shirt up and covered his nose. Bartholomew brayed again, more loudly. *HAW!*

Thomas grasped Bartholomew's reins and gave the donkey a tug. Bartholomew stepped cautiously forward one step, then two—and stopped again. He tried to shake his muzzle free of the reins and bawled, *Haw!*

"I know, I know," said Thomas. "Something is amiss. We need to find out what it is, and why the air is so foul." He pulled on Bartholomew again. The donkey dug his hooves into the spongy soil, sat back on his rump, and refused to move.

"Bartholomew! I need you to come with me," Thomas pleaded. It was no use. The donkey refused to take another step.

Thomas sighed. "All right. You wait here." He tied Bartholomew's reins to the broken end of a branch from a shrubby willow. Then he stroked the donkey's side to soothe him. "I'll just scout ahead a bit and see what's what."

Thomas, with Starfast raised, slipped quietly along the trampled path. The solid ground had given way to marshland. Impossibly thick grasses swayed on tall stalks above his head. Water had pooled in the sunken impressions left by the king's men and Heartwind. They must be close ahead. With each step the stink of rancid fish, rotting vegetation, and something else—he hated to think *what*—grew stronger until he thought he might gag. He did not stop.

He tried thinking of sweet smells to thwart the stench. He thought of the evening primroses in his mother's garden. When night came, the flowers opened and their perfume wafted through the open door. He thought of the smell coming from the brick oven when his family baked bread. He recalled how the castle kitchens smelled just before suppertime, when the juices from moist roasts fell into the hot ashes and sizzled. In this way he kept himself from crying out in fear.

Finally, he came to the turning of the trail. He touched Starfast lightly to his forehead, took a breath of the rot-infused air, and stepped out.

What met Thomas's startled eyes was the sight of a bubbling pool. It was neither wide nor long. But for all its daintiness, it was not a place to linger. All about were upturned boulders and trees ripped live from their moorings. Their shriveled roots looked somehow startled.

Aghast, Thomas left the path and made his way to the edge of the water. He glanced across, hoping to see the king on the other shore. He knew they were not far ahead, and the king's trail seemed to skirt the lake. As he stood there, a great bubble rose from the depths. It burst and filled the air with a vaporous cloud smelling of sulfur—and that other smell Thomas had not wanted to name—the stink of death.

chapter 12

When the cloud rained its reek
on him, Thomas staggered. He knew without a
doubt that this must be the lake the hill folk had
spoken of in their frightening tales. It had to be
the den of the many-headed beast of the lake—the
very place Thomas had hoped to avoid.

Thomas's stomach gave a lurch, and his arms
felt sickly and limp. Still, he gripped Starfast with
both hands. There was no avoiding the lake now.
He raised his sword high and declared, "This is
the way of my path, for good or ill. Beast of
the depths, I mean you no harm. Disturb me at
your peril!"

With that, Thomas exhaled and prepared to turn back to the king's trail, but he discovered that while he had stood on the shore, his feet had sunk into the muck. He was already buried to his shins. He felt the greedy suck of quicksand. "No!"

Quickly sheathing Starfast, he grabbed at one of his legs with both hands and tried to pull it up. Instead, he was sinking faster and was now buried to his knees. "No!" he cried again, struggling against his sinking. His violent wriggling only made it worse.

Not like this! I don't want to die like this! He forgot what to do to free himself from quicksand.

In his blind panic he did not see a tentacle flick up from the water and explore the lip of the lake. Therefore, it was with a shock that he felt the muscular arm of the beast wrap around his chest. Thomas had only seconds to draw Starfast from its sheath. He jabbed his sword into the fleshy tentacle up to its hilt and yanked it back out.

The pool bubbled over with black bile. The long arm unwrapped itself, swung around, and slapped Thomas into the air and down into the muck.

As he lay on his side in the mud and the ooze

from the wounded beast, Thomas's first thought was *I still have Starfast.* His second thought was *I'm free of the quicksand!* Immediately he flipped onto his stomach and began to slither away from the lake as quickly as he could without letting his knees and elbows sink in.

He'd gotten only a short distance from the shore when the tentacle whipped out again and caught Thomas around the waist. It dragged him back toward the water. There, several muck-crowned heads were rising from the depths. Thomas slashed at the beast as it lifted him. He took only a quick look at the greedy mouths that were snapping on the heads of the beast.

With each cut Starfast made, Thomas felt the beast quiver, he heard the waters rumble, and he smelled the dizzying reek of polluted outrage. Into his mind flashed his mother affectionately calling him stubborn. And then he remembered the day he'd met the king in the castle. He had waited hour after hour in the long, lonely corridor, holding on to hope. That hope had led to the king's bestowing his knighthood.

He held on to hope now. He took a deep breath and methodically stabbed and dragged Starfast through the tentacle. He didn't really want to kill the monster; he wanted to get free. The only way to do that was not to give up. Stubbornly, Thomas and Starfast did not give up, even as the water churned around them and the beast pulled him toward its hungry mouths.

Thomas went underwater. In the inky vastness, he sensed an evil beyond his understanding. It was an old evil—and he was young and afraid. Still, in the bright, hard knot of his mind, he would not stop fighting. Patiently, repeatedly, Starfast plunged into the flesh of the beast.

Thomas was drawing upon the last thin pockets of air in his lungs when he was thrust above the waves. He coughed out water and sucked in air. Then he gagged. He had inhaled the stench from a mouth filled with jagged teeth. It was close to his face.

It wasn't a terribly large mouth, and there was a gap between the teeth along one side. Suddenly Thomas knew what had to be done. He prayed that he and Starfast would be small enough to do it.

Thomas aimed, and—all in one smooth movement—he thrust his arm and Starfast straight through the tight gap in the beast's mouth. He twisted Starfast upright, yanked the sword back toward him, and wedged it between the creature's jaws.

As Thomas pulled his arm out, he felt a tremor pass through the tentacle that was holding him. The head bobbing before him, with Starfast lodged in its mouth, shuddered and began to jerk about, biting down on the sword. The other heads that had been coming at him from all sides began to pull back and sink below the surface.

The last thing Thomas heard as he, too, was

pulled under was a loud cracking sound that reverberated across the lake. The last thing he saw was Starfast's iron shaft flying out of the creature's bloody mouth and splashing into the dark water. The hilt had been bitten off and was jammed tightly into the gap in the creature's teeth.

At least I've wounded it, he thought. *It's going away to die.*

Beneath the water, Thomas was growing faint. He couldn't remember why there was sludge in his eyes, in his mouth, in his nose. He couldn't remember why he couldn't breathe. Thomas's last thought was *Perhaps I don't need to breathe?*

chapter 13

With a burst of energy that shook him all the way down to his bones, Thomas shot into the air. The beast had thrown him out of the lake.

Thomas landed with a thud in the shallows. The mud in his lungs slapped out of him. *Now* he fought for air, coughing and gasping to get the tiniest whiff, even as it pained him to breathe. He lay in the mucky shallows and groaned. He opened his eyes briefly when he felt himself being tugged sideways onto firmer soil. He saw two blurry figures looking down at him, blocking out the sky.

When his chest hurt a little less and he could breathe a little easier, Thomas tried opening his eyes and steadying his gaze. What he saw surprised him. Bartholomew and Jon were looking down at him with concern.

He closed his eyes, breathed deeply, and opened them again. This time no one was looking down at him. *I must have dreamed it,* Thomas thought. *Maybe I'm dead. If so, I might as well rest.* He rolled onto his side and slept.

Later he blinked, and there they were again— both of them. He struggled to speak. "Wha-a-t—" He could not make his mouth work right.

Jon leaned over him and wiped his forehead with a rag. "You're among the living, my friend Thomas," he said. "Here, drink this."

Thomas felt his head being lifted. He took a sip of something soothing. He took a second sip. Jon lowered his head gently. Above Thomas, Bartholomew's muzzle loomed hugely, as though the donkey were sniffing him to make sure he was all right. Then he proceeded to nibble a bit of grass by Thomas's ear.

It made Thomas want to smile, but he hurt too

much to do that. Instead, he simply whispered, "Bartholomew," and looked up at the clouds. He was suddenly happy listening to the loud, ordinary chomping sound of Bartholomew grazing by his ear. He was alive!

He ran his tongue over his lips. Feeling better, he slowly turned his head to find Jon. Instantly, the happiness in his heart died. Jon was also caring for another, who was resting farther back from the trail—it was the king!

Thomas struggled to rise, and Jon came scurrying back to him, exclaiming, "No, not yet. You're too weak to get up."

"But it's . . . it's the king!"

Jon nodded. "Yes." His chin quivered. "He's sleeping."

"What happened?"

Jon spoke softly. "We're all that's left. That . . ." He pointed to the water. "That *thing* surprised us as we were hacking a path around the far side of the lake. All these . . . these long arms came out and scooped up several of us before we—" He put his hands over his eyes. His whole body shook for a moment before he could continue. "The king had his sword, and we had pikes and staffs! Still, we were no match for that . . . that . . ." Jon trailed off, shaking his head.

Thomas could only too well imagine what it had been like. He felt his stomach cramping, but he forced himself to ask, "Where . . . why is the king riding out?"

"The princess!" said Jon. "Not long after you left, he stormed along the battlements and across the grounds, saying he would not send children out to do what men should do. He declared that any who would follow him would be well rewarded. Then he left Marshal Wattley in charge until some of the knights should return.

"I do not blame him," added Jon. "He fears for his daughter's life. So eight from the castle who were fit enough for the journey left with him. I pleaded with him to take me so I could care for Heartwind, but he said I was too young. I told him I had almost thirteen years, but still he wouldn't!"

"Jon!" Thomas swallowed, and then he sighed. "You've not got but twelve, if that."

"Well," Jon said with a shrug, "you know me. I'm a conspirator and the new assistant under-groomsman, after all. So I packed myself up, plucked a few apples for the journey, and joined the king two days later. He wanted to send me back on my own, but I told him I could track Bartholomew's hoofprints anywhere. I've been a big help! We tracked you for a good part of the way.

"Of course, all the people we met told us which way you were headed anyway. But I didn't let that get between me and being useful to the king. Then there weren't any more people to ask and we got ahead of you somehow."

"I saw you ride by, up in the highlands," said Thomas. "I tried to catch up, but Bartholomew . . ."

Jon nodded and looked over at the donkey, who was still grazing nearby. A shadow of a smile played about his mouth. Almost immediately it hardened into a thin line, and Jon squeezed his eyes tight. "We fought that thing, Thomas, we did! Even old Timothy the gardener, who would not stay behind. I was knocked backward and flew into the tall grasses. Heartwind . . . Oh! It was horrible." Tears spilled from Jon's eyes. "When I came to, I found the king sheltered under . . .

under Heartwind. It took all the strength I had, but I pulled him out."

"Is he terribly hurt?" asked Thomas, attempting to rise.

"Easy . . . ," Jon said. He took Thomas by the shoulders to help him sit upright. "Yes. But he's still sleeping. He needs his rest. I dragged him away from that place and followed our trail back through the thicket to here, where we found you. I heard splashing. I—"

Suddenly Jon put his hand over his mouth and scrambled up. Thomas could hear him gagging nearby. When Jon returned, it was in a choked whisper that he added, "All those heads and arms came back to grab whatever was left on the shore. It spared none, not even . . . not even my Heartwind!"

"Oh, Jon!" Thomas's heart ached for his friend, and for the great horse. Still, he stole a quick glance over his shoulder, toward the lake.

"We do not need to fear now. Look." Jon pointed at the lake. There was no sign of any of the heads. "I think it's dead. And the waters are stilled."

Several long tentacles trailed limply over tree trunks on the shore, already making a feast for vultures and ravens. Thomas saw that at least one of the tentacles had been shredded by a hundred tiny sword thrusts.

chapter 14

Thoughts of the ancient evil that
Thomas felt in the depths of the lake returned. He
sat forward and put his head in his hands. After a
few moments, he looked up and stared at the
water. "I've lost Starfast," he told Jon. His mouth
scrunched up. He had to stop his jaw from quivering before he spoke again. "How can I rescue the
princess without a sword, Jon? Some champion
I've made!"

"What happened to it?"

"The beast bit the hilt off when I stuck it in its
mouth. I saw the shaft fly into the water."

Jon whistled. "You stuck Starfast in one of
its mouths?"

Thomas nodded.

"You got close enough to kill it that way?" Jon asked again, as though he hadn't heard it right the first time.

"I think so. But before it died, it threw me out of the water."

Jon leaned over and laid his palm on Thomas's brow. "You're hot. I think you're fevered and talking crazy. Why would that beast throw you out of the lake? You need to rest some more."

"It did!" Thomas said. Then he was silent for a moment, staring at the limp tentacles on the shore. And so quietly that Jon barely heard him, Thomas added, "It's strange. One of the last things I remember seeing before I began to sink was Starfast's hilt. It was stuck in the jagged gap of those teeth like . . . I know this will sound crazy, but it seemed to me like it fit, like it belonged there. . . ."

Jon shook his head and laid a hand on each of Thomas's shoulders. "Why don't you lie back down? You're starting to sound as wild as those people from the foothills who told us the strangest stor—" He stopped. "Wait! They were *right* about the beast of many heads that lived here." He let go of Thomas and sat down by his side. "And there was something else. The monster wanted something given back to it. But what?"

"Something that had been taken away from it," Thomas said. "They told me the same strange tales. I thought they just wanted to frighten me."

"Little did they know you, or Starfast," said Jon, smiling. Then he sat thoughtfully chewing the inside of his lip.

"What?" asked Thomas.

"Well, I think I may be light-headed, too. But . . . I was just thinking about Starfast. Didn't you say its hilt was ivory? That's a tooth, right?"

"Yes. Or a tusk. Like a whale's tooth, or a—" Thomas suddenly stopped and turned to face Jon. He whispered, "Or a . . . tooth from an ancient beast!" Then he pointed at the pool. "I did feel something very, very old in there."

"Remember the swordsmith who carved the hilt?" added Jon. "He told Sir Gerald it could only be for the giving, not the taking, or something like that. Well, you gave it back."

"Did I? The hill folk said the creature would only be defeated if it got back that which was taken from it." Thomas thought for a moment.

"Sir Gerald said the tooth had been found in a fish. So . . . do you think that's what happened? That somehow a fish from this lake took the tooth that became Starfast's hilt?"

Jon nodded, his eyes wide.

"And I gave it"—Thomas's voice slid down to a whisper—"I gave it back when I thrust Starfast into its mouth." Thomas rose shakily to his feet. "But I didn't mean to kill it, Jon! I just couldn't let it kill me. I . . ."

"Maybe you didn't kill it," said Jon.

"What do you mean? It looks dead."

They both stared at the tentacles being picked at by the flock of birds.

Jon shrugged as he rose from the ground. "Maybe those stories from the hills . . . maybe they meant that the creature was just waiting to get its tooth back, and then it could die. You know? I mean, now that it was all in one piece. And it was old, you said."

Thomas was silent, thinking about this. Then he turned to glance at the king lying behind them. "If only I had gotten to the lake first, before the king."

At that, Jon grabbed hold of his friend and gave

him a shake. "Stop! Stop that. You couldn't have prevented that thing from attacking us. We can't see the future. And, well . . . well, *I* wouldn't want to foresee all the times *I'm* sure to get into trouble, anyway. Just be thankful you had Bartholomew with you."

"Bartholomew?" Thomas asked.

"Yes. He found you. I was helping the king back along the way we'd come. I heard splashing in the water. I thought it was the beast eating . . ." He paused. "I couldn't see anything until we rounded a thicket and I saw Bartholomew charge right out on this spit of land. He shook his head and brayed. I was so worried about the king that I might not have seen you lying here if Bartholomew hadn't made sure of it."

Thomas looked at the aged donkey and remembered that Bartholomew hadn't wanted to follow him down to the water's edge. Earlier, he'd sat down and refused to budge.

Thomas might have lost Starfast in the depths of the lake—but he still had his trusty mount. He wanted to give Bartholomew a good hug.

Despite his muddy hands, Thomas took hold of

Bartholomew's old gray muzzle and looked him in the eyes. "Thank you," he said. Bartholomew twirled his ears forward and bawled softly, *Ha-a-a.*

"And thank you for taking such care of my shield." Thomas untied his buckler from Bartholomew's belt.

Jon said, "Should we look for Starfast's shaft? You said it was flung away when the hilt got bitten off."

"No." Thomas shook his head. "Let us see to the king. Perhaps he has awakened."

The king was worse off than Thomas had thought. He was having difficulty breathing.

Jon had set him down to rest in the tall grasses off the trail. He had covered him with some bloodied clothes retrieved from their battle on the lakeshore.

Thomas knelt at the king's side. "Sire," he whispered, "it is I, Sir Thomas."

Slowly the king's eyes opened. Thomas could see that the king was trying to smile. Instead, he winced and said, "Despite the mud you wear, good knight, I would have recognized you."

"How does my liege fare?"

"Not well, Thomas. Yet these wounds are naught compared to the hurt in my heart. My desire to save my only child has led to the deaths of good men, and to the death of the loyal steed Heartwind." The king squeezed his eyes shut and whispered, "So rash! So rash! I'm such an old fool. I should have waited for the return of my knights."

The king drew several shaky breaths and opened his eyes again before he continued. "And you . . . I was ashamed that I'd sent one new knight, so young, out to do what I should have been doing! When I was younger, I rescued several princesses. I had to try to rescue my own daughter."

Slowly the king turned his head toward the lake. "Jon tells me you killed the many-headed beast." Then he did manage a slight smile before adding, "That is well done. Well done. . . ." The king's voice trailed off weakly.

Thomas surveyed the lakeshore, too. He made up his mind. The king needed to be somewhere dry and warm. "Sire," he said, "we need to get you to a place of rest where you may be rightly cared for."

The king nodded absently.

"If you will allow us, Jon and I shall lift you up onto Bartholomew. There is a ruined cottage a short way back. It is a sad place, but dry, and you may safely spend the night. Close beyond, not more than a day's ride, is a farm with a good widow who will surely help. I stopped there and she fed me well. It is not far, my lord."

Jon and Sir Thomas lifted their wounded king onto Bartholomew and, using strips of cloth torn from the things Jon had scavenged after the beast had attacked them, they tied the king securely to the donkey. His feet dragged upon the ground; there was no help for that.

While Jon strapped on the king's sword, Thomas took his bag of provisions and fished out one wrapped packet of bread from the few that remained. At the bottom of the pouch, his fingers touched something. Carefully he withdrew the hard object. In his hand was a small wooden horse, its mane carved as though it was leaping into the air. It was Isabel's toy, the horse his father had carved when she was just a baby. He clutched it in his hand. She had slipped it into his pouch the day he'd left home. He felt his heart lift.

He put the piece of wrapped bread and Isabel's

toy into his pocket. The rest he gave to Jon, telling him he must take it to feed himself and the king until they got to the widow's farm. "And you'll need this as well, since you did not retrieve the king's standard. It will ensure your safe passage." He handed Jon his shield with Sir Gerald's and the king's coat of arms upon it.

"Aren't you going also?" asked Jon.

Thomas shook his head. "The king has entrusted me with rescuing Princess Eleanor. He cannot do that; I must. I know you will tend to the king as though he were Heartwind himself." Thomas smiled. "And you'll have the brave Bartholomew with you."

Thomas nodded toward the far shore. "My way lies around the lake, to the sea and Barren Isle."

Thomas lifted the reins his father had made for Bartholomew. He touched the leather lightly with one finger. "Jon, after you return to the castle, send word to my family that I'm well. And tell Isabel thank you for sharing."

He handed the reins to Jon, stroked Bartholomew between his eyes, and scratched the top of the donkey's head. "I will miss you, my traveling companion." The words caught in his throat. "But I'll be back, soon, to visit both you and the new assistant under-groomsman in the stables."

Bartholomew nudged Sir Thomas with his nose.

As Jon led the donkey back along the trail, Thomas raised a hand and waved to his friends. Bartholomew stopped once and turned toward Thomas, and then he trotted off bearing his wounded king upon his back.

chapter 15

As his friends rounded a bend in the trail, Thomas lowered his hand and rested it on his filthy chest. "So now I have neither a sword nor a steed," he said aloud, and shook his head. "Some champion I've made."

Beneath the mud, Thomas could feel the leather jerkin his father had made him. *Well, I still have my jerkin,* he thought. *Perhaps, with its protection, I can get close enough to the dragon to rescue the princess.*

But right now Thomas stank so much, he could hardly stand it. However, he did not want to touch the spoiled waters of the lake again. He wanted nothing more than to get far from that dismal place.

He was sore and bone-tired. Carefully skirting the quicksand of the shore where he'd stood earlier, he made his way steadily—if not as swiftly as he would have liked—along the trail the king's men had blazed ahead of him around the lake.

He came to the spot where the king and his men had fought the beast. Thomas saw long drag marks disappearing into the lake. There were dark stains on the upturned boulders and on the sand. Bits and pieces of clothing littered the shore. His stomach felt queasy. However, he did not pause except to look quickly about for any sign of the king's standard. He saw only a strip of the blue flag floating on the water.

Along the way he kept a keen eye out for the iron shaft from Starfast. He did not find it.

From this point forward Thomas had to forge his own route around the lake, breaking through the dense tangle of shrubs and grasses. Without a sword to hack at the growth, or Bartholomew to stomp down a path, it was slow going. Yet Thomas found that his smallness helped him slip easily beneath branches and past the sharp edges of grass that could slice through skin. Many a time, the padded jerkin protected him. By late afternoon, he'd made it to the far side. A slender shoulder of dune and a pebbled beach were all that separated the sea from the tangled thicket at the back of the lake.

Coming over the dune, Sir Thomas heard pounding, like a giant heartbeat knocking against his ribs. Then he saw the sea for the first time in his life. There were rumbling waves rolling in and in, beating mercilessly at the shore.

The endlessness of the blue water meeting the blue sky frightened him. After the gloomy lake, it hurt his eyes. If he squinted hard enough, however, he might be able to see the farther shore of the bay. He could hardly believe that there was a place where the world simply disappeared into the horizon.

He shielded his face and looked toward the westering sun. Not far in that direction, there was something he couldn't miss—a dark shape. Just down the shore, sitting in the entrance from the ocean to the bay, was an island with two mountains

like jagged brown teeth. It had to be Barren Isle. He wrapped his arms around his chest to stop his shivering.

Thomas made his way down the dune to the shingle on the shore. He dipped his hands into the waves that rushed up to meet him. The air tasted salty. The water was salty. He knew it was supposed to be, but it surprised him nevertheless.

He tried to wash some of the muck from his face and body. Then he sat down and nibbled a tiny bit of his remaining bread. He carefully rewrapped the rest and tucked it deep into his pocket with Isabel's horse. All the while he wondered how he was going to get across the water to the island.

Thomas had been thinking about this for some time along the journey. He'd thought there'd be some sort of boat when he got to the shore, or a cottager who would row him out to the island. Truthfully, though, it did not surprise him that no one seemed to live this close to the awful lake and the dragons of Barren Isle.

Thomas decided he'd better have a look around before the sun set and darkness came on. He did not relish the idea of sleeping with the lake at his back. He hoped he'd find someplace a bit more sheltered. He trod off along the shore in the direction of Barren Isle.

In a short while, Thomas noticed a humped spit of land that stuck out from the seashore. As he drew closer, it became obvious that it was a long wall of rocks, like a bony finger stabbing into the sea. The tip was a goodly way off, and it was difficult to make out its details. However, it seemed to Thomas that there was a crook in the wall. Near the tip, gray waves crashed furiously.

When Thomas arrived at the spot where the rocky causeway branched off, he could see that it did, indeed, have a crook near the tip. Now the assembled boulders looked like a beckoning finger. Thomas wondered to whom it was beckoning. The causeway jutted so far out that there couldn't be much distance between the tip and the shallows around Barren Isle. Did it serve as the invitation to dragons on the isle to ravage the countryside? Or did it point the way for travelers to explore the dragons' island—a trap, perhaps?

Sir Thomas did not like the look of it. However,

night was coming on and he had no place to wait for the day except upon one of the sun-heated slabs of stone. At least it would be warm for a short while from the sunshine it had absorbed, and dry.

He scrambled a little distance along the rocky finger and found a spot where he could lie between two up-thrusting walls of granite and not worry about rolling off. He lay on his side, head cradled in his hand, and pulled his knees up. As he drifted toward sleep, he thought about snuggling down into the good, clean hay of the sleeping loft back home. He thought about blanket tugs-o'-war with his brothers, about the stories Da told, and about his own bedtime boasting: *One day I'll be a knight and ride off on a quest for the king.* Oh, if he'd only known how lonely and bone-wearying it was!

He allowed himself a small smile. What a story the beast of the lake would make to tell his brothers and sisters. What a tale to tell Da! Albert would be sure to catch every word of it. He was certain of that.

He slid his free hand into his pocket until it

touched the wooden horse. He imagined Isabel's bright laughter. In the deepening dark a new thought came to him. Perhaps—just perhaps—his hand and his heart would be strong enough for what lay ahead.

Book IV

Tilting Toward Doom

chapter 16

Thomas awoke damp and sore, still aching from the fight with the beast of the lake. He winced. Sleeping all night on hard stone hadn't helped. At first he couldn't get his legs and feet to work properly. He feared sliding off a boulder and into the sea, so he took some time to stretch and to nibble a tiny bite from the remaining bread. Then he shut his eyes and soaked up a bit of morning sunshine on his face. Eventually there was nothing more to do but to go on. And there was only one way to go, toward the end of the rocky causeway.

Thomas began to pick his way up, over, around,

and down the huge boulders. Like a spider, he clung gingerly to the slopes of stones he could not see over, and imagined they must have been tossed there by giants. As he ventured along toward the tip, the out-thrusting finger of land grew skinnier and taller.

Choppy waves rocked up and splashed over him, though he tried to stay near the crest of the jumbled boulders. In addition, he was beginning to notice more and more gaps between the stones. These crevices gurgled, filled with water as a wave came in and then drained away, gulping to unknown depths. What if he should fall and slip into one?

All this water washing the slanted sides of the boulders made for precarious footholds. More than once he put a foot or hand down only to find he was sliding and had to throw himself backward. It was a long and arduous route that required all of Thomas's concentration. Therefore, he was surprised when, climbing on his knees to a ledge, he found himself at the crook of the rocky finger.

Here waves funneled in through a narrow slit

open to the sea at both ends. Across the gap continued the rocky finger of land for a short distance before sloping off into the depths. In this water-filled gorge were massed knots of old netting, wood that might have once been boats, and bleached tree trunks. The whole mishmash was continually bashed against the boulders on both halves of the causeway. The roaring of the water and the banging of the logs was so loud that Thomas had to put his hands over his ears as he surveyed the water-filled trench between him and the other side.

Somehow he had to get from this stony point out to Barren Isle. When he'd first seen the causeway, he thought it ended close to the island, and he'd nursed the small hope that he might be able to wade across. That had been an illusion, for the closer he got to the tip of the finger of land, the farther away the island seemed to be. He shook his head. Despite the drenching he was getting from the splashing waves, he lay down on his stomach, hung his head over the side, and took a closer look into the watery gap. Perhaps there might be something washed into it that he could use to strike out across the bay toward the island? After all he'd been through, he wouldn't allow himself to stop now.

Caught up in his thoughts about getting to the island, Sir Thomas almost did not see the silvery fin waving from below. However, upon rising, he saw a flash in the rocks, slightly to the side of the slit and below a high-water mark that had stained the rocks the length of the causeway.

At first he thought it might be a piece of snagged metal. But as he stared at it, it seemed to move of its own accord—not in rhythm with the waves.

Thomas lay down again, brushed his wet hair aside, and squinted through cupped hands. He spied a beautiful creature. He had never seen one before—except those that were woven into the artwork of the tapestries that hung in the castle. He was certain it was a dolphin. Thomas had spent much of his spare time with the other boys at the castle studying the animals in the tapestries.

This one was trapped in tangled netting. Every time a wave rushed in, the poor creature banged up against a rock. Then the receding water would uncover the dolphin to the air and wind. Thomas was surprised the animal was still alive. He leaned forward, as far as he dared, and stared into its eyes—they were wild with fright. It called out. To him? Was the creature calling to Thomas for help?

Thomas surveyed the choppy waters nearby. Another fin was slicing through the waves—and then a sleek silver back curved up. It was a larger dolphin, and it was circling nearby. Thomas watched it raise its snout above the waves and squeal, as though in answer to the one caught in the net.

Thomas wiped the water from his face. He ducked his head and peered as closely as he could at the smaller, trapped dolphin. Why, it was just a baby!

It cried out again. Was the circling one its mother?

In his astonishment at the scene before him, Thomas found he'd hardly dared to breathe. Now his breath came back to him in a painful rush. The trapped dolphin was a baby—he had to do something! He had to do it fast before the baby was pounded to death on the rocks.

Still, Thomas closed his eyes for a moment to steady himself. He remembered with some shame his panic in the quicksand. If he had calmed down and thought about his situation—about how to lie back and float on top of the quicksand—he might not have been dragged into the lake.

Thomas opened his eyes and came up with a plan. He glanced along the side of the causeway and saw several logs there as well. Some were tossed higher than the other debris—above the rushing water. With great care, Thomas slithered down the steep decline of the boulders.

Finally, he made it to the top of a rock near the logs. There he found a smaller branch, which he used to roll one of the longer logs over several times, until it slid forward a short distance and wedged itself down into a cranny. Thomas lay on his stomach, wrapped his arms around the log, and scooted down the slippery length of it to a mound of floating timbers and litter below.

One of the young dolphin's eyes bulged watchfully as Thomas balanced himself upon the half-submerged pyramid of small logs and wave-tossed debris. The distressed creature was caught on the side of the raft that was closest to the channel and was covered in dirty foam. Fortunately, Thomas was so light that he did not sink through the rocking, floating hodgepodge.

Carefully he lay down across the raft of litter and reached out to the tangled creature at the water's edge. A wave crashed over him; he slammed his eyes shut. A minute later, he gulped for air. When he did, he glanced up and saw the larger dolphin close by, as though watching his every move. He began to work on the knots ensnaring her baby.

chapter 17

Thomas's fingers were small and the rope of the net was large. The net was also water-soaked and heavy. He hadn't the strength to haul it up. So, patiently, he endured the battering waves as they regularly rose and slapped over him, only stopping to breathe deeply when he needed to steady himself. He pried at knots with a small stick he found in the debris, he bit through twine and grasses bound up with the net when he had to, and when he was so tired he could barely continue, he noticed that he was lying lower in the water. He looked over his shoulder. The back end of his floating raft was rising. It was now closer to the high-water mark that had stained the rocks.

The tide was coming in. Thomas had learned about tides in his studies, about how they came and went. When tides were low, clammers could walk out on the exposed sand. When they rose, water covered the mudflats. That must be what was happening now: the waters were rising. Though his tangled platform still floated, its front edge dipped at a sharper angle into the sea. It was getting caught up in the larger logs that littered the causeway. And the dolphin caught in the net was sinking below the water, farther from Thomas's reach. There were no more cries from it. At this slow pace, Thomas would fail and the young one would die.

He needed something to cut the net, but he no longer had Starfast. If only he had a piece of metal, something with an edge or point! He could see one bit of shiny metal snagged in the rocks, but there was no reaching that. He tucked his wet, numb hands into his armpits to warm them for a moment and to think. That's when his hand brushed one of the clasps on his leather jerkin.

Metal, Thomas realized. He'd completely forgotten that he had metal clasps on his jacket. He slid back to a more stable position and slipped his jerkin off. Quickly he unfastened the clasps and wiggled out of the vest.

Again it took his breath away. How light and supple it was! How beautifully fashioned were the clasps! Da was a master craftsman, and Thomas doubted there would be any sharp bits on the intricate clasps, or any easy way to break one off and sharpen part of it—but he had to try. Time was running out. The anxious mother dolphin was calling repeatedly. Getting no response, she was circling frantically, too close to the pull of the watery fissure between the rocks. Thomas was afraid she might get sucked into that melee.

Nimbly Thomas ran his fingers over the clasps, inspecting every bend of them. He tried to find a bit he could wiggle until he could break one of them off, with no success. He was just about to give up when something pricked his finger. "Ouch!" A drop of blood appeared.

He brushed the water from his eyes, held the jerkin up close to his face, and searched for what had poked him. Near the top of the bottom clasp, a small circle of silver had been broken and twisted outward. *It must have happened in the struggle with the beast,* thought Thomas.

It was just what he needed. He crawled forward, clutching the jerkin. The whole floating pile of litter tilted abruptly downward. His head went into the water; he yanked it back, sputtering. "Ah!"

Thomas wedged his knees between some sturdy branches in the pile and hooked a foot over a thin log. He could no longer see the trapped young dolphin. He plunged a hand into the sea and felt for the netting. With his other hand, he fisted up the leather of the jacket, with the broken piece of metal pointing out, and began to saw at the tangles.

As soon as he cut through one strand, he grabbed for another and another. Now his shoulders were lying in the water and he was having a hard time keeping his balance. The timbers on the floating pile were shifting with the rising tide and starting to float apart. Thomas strained to keep his head out of the water. His neck muscles ached. His arms ached.

However, he could feel that the knotted net

was becoming looser. He saw it start to float up and gape open. Suddenly the silver fin of the small dolphin flashed to the surface. The mother cried loudly, dipping her head, circling more and more tightly. The young one was straining at the net with its muscled back. It touched Thomas's hands as it struggled, and he could feel its panic. Thomas grabbed and sawed at whatever netting he could reach.

He gulped air just before a huge wave hit. It almost knocked him from his perch. When it hit, he thought of his struggle with the beast. He thought of his own young brothers and sisters when they were frightened—the idea that this baby might die tore at his heart.

With that thought, he sucked in all the air he could and threw himself into the next wave, lunging and grabbing at the net. He rose between waves, spit out the salt water, inhaled again, and dove back beneath the surface—sawing through the last bit of knot. When he did, hunks of netting flew up against the rocks. The baby surfaced, arching above the waves. The mother dolphin rose into the air. And the raft Thomas floated on washed apart.

Thomas slid into the sea.

He was shocked by his sudden sinking. Not so much by the cold water, for he was already drenched from head to toe, but by how completely he'd forgotten about his own perilous position. He had concentrated so fiercely upon rescuing the young dolphin that now *he* needed rescuing!

He kept a tight grip on his jerkin, and the cork within it helped him float back to the surface. But the waves kept pulling him under and out, and he had a hard time keeping his head above water. When he could, Thomas gasped for air. He kicked wildly, trying to get back to the rocks but not be smashed against them.

Then he was hurled sideways by a wave—not toward land, but toward the channel in the crook of the causeway. Soon he'd be caught in that awful undertow and hauled into the gorge, where he'd be pounded and smashed in the whirlpool of trapped logs. He shook the wet hair from his eyes and, stretching out his arms and legs for all he was worth, attempted to swim toward shore. One leg went kicking down and back. It hit something.

Something silver-smooth glided up and under

him. The mother dolphin raised him above the waves.

Thomas hooked his jerkin over the dolphin's dorsal fin. Clinging to the leather vest, he managed to pull himself across the creature's broad back. Then he collapsed.

chapter 18

When Sir Thomas had enough of his strength back to raise his head and look around, he saw the dolphin's snout cutting through the waves just below the surface. Then he realized, with relief, that his leather vest remained securely over its fin. He sighed. *I still have my jerkin.* Also, he saw that the young dolphin dove and leapt alongside them. Thomas smiled and rested his cheek against the mother's strong body. After watching the young one for a while, Thomas looked beyond the mother toward the horizon and noticed they were heading out to sea!

He swiveled about, trying to stay balanced

across the slippery back of the dolphin. He clasped the fin and peered over his shoulder. They were passing by the island of the dragons. The red rocks of Barren Isle's peaks thrust up out of the water just a short distance to his right. "Wait! Wait!" he cried, yanking on his rescuer's fin.

The great creature slowed and fanned its tail about in the water, turning in circles for a moment, as though wondering what this thing on her back wanted. "Closer," said Thomas, for he feared he had only a little strength left to get to the island.

Thomas did not know if the creature understood him, but he slid partway off. Hanging from one side and holding tightly on to the fin with both hands, he tried to tug the dolphin in the direction he wanted to go. "This way!"

The dolphin slowed and circled again—inward, toward Thomas. Thomas continued tugging at her fin. She circled again and again, toward this thing she had picked up. With each circle the animal drew closer and closer to Barren Isle until Thomas said, "Yes! Here. Here. This is good."

Still grasping the creature's fin with one hand,

Thomas slid down and touched sandy bottom. He reached out with his free hand to lift his vest from the fin, but the dolphin suddenly dove, jerking away from Thomas. She swam into the distance, the leather jerkin fluttering from her fin.

"My jerkin!" Thomas screamed. "Come back, that's mine!"

His vest floated free of the dolphin's fin for a moment. *Maybe I can still get to it,* Thomas thought. He was about to attempt the swim when he felt something nudge his leg. He looked down in time to see the baby swim past him, leap from the water, and snag Thomas's jerkin on his snout!

"Bring it here!" Thomas yelled.

The young one carried it farther out. He tossed it in the air and dove under. His mother came up nearby and batted it with her tail flukes. In disbelief, Thomas saw his cork vest fly through the air. They were playing with it!

Thomas felt another nudge at his side. Then the baby surfaced some distance away and chattered to him.

"I can't swim out that far," he cried. They had batted his vest between them and had carried it a long way into the bay. It was no use. As he watched, he could see the occasional fin or flash of silver back as the pair continued to play. Thomas sighed. The dolphins had stolen the gift from his da, and it would only be a matter of minutes before they, and his beautiful leather jerkin, were out of the bay and at sea.

Thomas dragged himself toward the rocky shore of the island. He'd lost everything. He no longer had Starfast, or his shield, or Bartholomew, or his jerkin! "Oh!" he groaned. Thomas was on the verge of tears.

He flung himself upon the coarse rusty red beach and didn't even care that the sunbaked rocks burned his bare chest. Perhaps they would burn into him all the way. *That would be good.* If his heart burned, maybe he wouldn't feel so bad about losing all the gifts others had entrusted to him.

He didn't allow himself to cry. *Knights don't cry.* Instead, he sniggered, making fun of his efforts. *No sword, no steed, and now no jerkin. Oh, what a champion I've made! I even lost my raggedy shirt in the water. Let's see, what have I left to use*

a-questing? He rolled over and sat up. From his
wet pockets he pulled out a clump of soggy bread
and Isabel's horse.

Aloud, he said, "Here! Here's a bit of wet bread
for your quest. Oh, and don't forget your valiant
toy steed. You'll need it." Then he slumped down
and thought about tossing these useless things as
far from him as he could.

He didn't. The truth was, he didn't have

enough energy to raise his arm and throw. He simply sat—ashamed and exhausted. Oh, he'd wrestled with the beast of the lake all right, and it had died. But what good was that? He hadn't even wanted it to die, not really. After all, he'd set out to rescue the princess, not to kill a monster.

What would his mother and father think of him? Surely it had cost his father dearly to get the cork and the silver for his jerkin. And what would Sir Gerald think? He'd prayed, and had entrusted Starfast to Thomas. Now Starfast was broken and lost. And what about the king when he heard of this failure? And . . . Isabel?

chapter 19

Thomas had not bothered to look around the beach where he sat. Bridgoltha could have been standing right behind him. He simply sat, slumped over, resigned to whatever might befall him. As he was completely unequipped, he was in no hurry to face anyone or anything. No one ever came back from Barren Isle, anyhow. He'd thought that, with the protection of the padded jerkin, he might at least be able to get close enough to a fire-breathing dragon to snatch Princess Eleanor away. Now what chance did he have of rescuing her?

He waited, praying in a dim, small part of his

heart for a dragon to creep up on him and devour him in a single gulp. Surely that wouldn't hurt so much—one swallow, and he'd be done for! He was so tired. At least getting eaten by a dragon would be a noble death. His parents and Sir Gerald could still be proud of him. The king could say that he'd bravely ventured forth . . . only to be lost forever.

Thomas waited while the sun rose overhead. Was it only midday? It seemed like it was hours ago that he'd worked to free the young dolphin. *How quickly one's fortunes can change.*

He remembered how relieved he'd been to survive the beast in the lake. Now he stuffed the wooden horse back into his pocket and absent-mindedly ate his soggy bread. It was the last of his food. He closed his eyes.

"Hello!" came a voice.

Thomas fairly jumped out of his skin! Someone was behind him. He scrambled to his feet and jerked around, his heart beating wildly. Whoever was there, it suddenly came to him that *maybe* he didn't want to die right this minute.

It wasn't a dragon. It was Princess Eleanor! Just as quickly as Thomas had jumped up and turned, he dropped to his knee and bowed his head. "My lady!" he cried.

Thomas heard some clunking noises as he kept his head bent. A moment later, a pleasant voice said, "You may look up."

Thomas lifted his eyes to the princess. At her feet sat two wooden buckets yoked to a strong pole. Her dress was tattered, and her dark hair was loose and wild about her head. Thomas only slowly took these details in, for he could not stop smiling at her. And she was happily smiling back. In his heart Thomas suddenly knew he would go—even bare-handed—to the ends of the earth to rescue her.

"Aren't you . . . Jon's friend Thomas?" she asked.

"I am Sir Thomas, a . . . a Knight of the Realm," he stuttered, suddenly shy.

"You're a knight now?" she exclaimed. Then, as though hurrying not to offend, she quickly added, "Excuse me, it's . . . Well, surely you're too young to be a knight, Thomas. Mayhap you're a squire?"

"I am but recently knighted, Your Highness."

"I see." Eleanor thought about this a moment, and looked past him. "Where are the others?"

"There are no others."

The princess was silent. Finally, she nodded. "The knights are still at the border, then?"

"Yes."

"I hope it goes well for them. I was on my way to seek help from our friends along the coast when the dragon queen stole me away and brought me here." Then she looked about the beach again and asked, "Where is your boat?"

Thomas had trouble swallowing. "I have none, my lady."

"And yet you are here." She paused. "On an island." She clasped her hands and waited for Thomas to answer.

"I . . . I rode here upon the back of a dolphin, Your Highness."

Eleanor raised an eyebrow. A short moment later, she said, "It is good to know we have such *resourceful* knights."

Thomas didn't think he should contradict a princess, but he didn't think he was very resourceful at all! He struggled with how to tell her of his failings, for he'd been raised to be truthful. He hung his head and said, "I'm not so sure the king would be proud of this knight. The dolphins took my floating jerkin from me. And my blade, Starfast, was broken and lost to the depths when I fought the beast of the lake." He heard a small gasp from the princess and looked up.

"Did you kill that monster?"

Thomas hesitated. Had he? Had he *really*? Or perhaps it was as Jon had said, that the beast simply died after getting its tooth back. "It had a small gap in its teeth on one of the heads. I wedged my sword into the gap. It bit the hilt off. And then it died."

Eleanor paused and seemed to look kindly at him as he knelt. She said, "On the journey here, we passed over that dismal lake and the stench made me ill. I felt the chill of evil myself. I doubt the king will be distressed about the loss of one sword now that the beast is dead."

Thomas gulped and almost broke into tears. "But it was not until *after* the king had been hurt."

"The king hurt!" cried Eleanor. She pulled him up firmly by his arm. "Arise, good knight, and tell me exactly what has happened!"

Thomas's limbs quivered as he stood close to the princess and stared into her fiery green eyes. "The king and some men from the castle grounds came to rescue you, my lady. They only got as far as that dismal pool. I was following behind them, and arrived too late. They'd already been attacked. But do not fear—the king lives. Heartwind gave his life protecting him. And Jon has led the king away to a place of safety, tied upon Bartholomew's back. I came onward to rescue you."

Eleanor let go of Thomas's arm. "Bartholomew?" she asked.

Sir Thomas explained, "He was my mount. I sent him to carry the king home."

The princess walked over to sit on a nearby rock. "Forgive me if I frightened you . . . Sir Thomas. I feared for my father's well-being. Now that I have heard your story, I think you must be proud of your quest thus far. Your stature has served you well."

Now it was Thomas's turn to raise an eyebrow. What did she mean by that? He didn't know what to say. It didn't *sound* as though the princess was making fun of how short he was.

Eleanor brushed back a lock of hair, and Thomas saw that her eyes were filling with tears. He relaxed.

"My friend Heartwind is no more?" asked the princess.

Thomas remembered how fond the princess had been of the king's warhorse. He nodded.

"I shall truly miss him. He was the bearer of many girlhood secrets that I often whispered in his ear. In return, he asked for only an apple or a pear. And I am sure that though my father's body is not completely broken, his heart is."

Thomas could barely speak. "And Jon's," he added quietly.

"Yes," the princess agreed. "Our Jon, too, will miss him." She paused for a moment, straightening her shoulders, and continued. "Well, I trust that Bartholomew's strong back will carry the king a long, steady way. There is no better mount for that duty. We are lucky Bartholomew was with you.

"And now you have ridden a dolphin to rescue me." She wiped at a last tear and laughed a soft laugh.

"La! Perhaps we shall ride a dolphin off the

island together? I have often watched their graceful playing in the bay. That would be a grand adventure for a princess."

Then Eleanor sighed and looked away. "Unfortunately," she said, "I will never be permitted to leave the island until we've dealt with the dragon. There's no running away from this one, or riding off on the back of a dolphin. That would make matters worse for everyone." The princess put her head in her hand, thinking. "Actually," she muttered, "there are thirteen dragons to be concerned about."

Thomas yelped, "Thirteen dragons!"

Book V

Trespass and Treasure

chapter 20

Thomas had trouble clearing his throat. Oh, how he wanted Starfast now, and Bartholomew, and the protection of his heavy jerkin! When he could speak again, he squeaked, "Thir-teen?" He lowered his voice. "Um, I mean . . . thirteen, my lady?"

"Yes," she said, studying him. "However, I assure you, Thomas"—she waved a hand dismissively—"twelve of them are quite small."

He nodded and took several quick glances over his shoulder. Getting swallowed in one gulp was one thing, he reasoned. But after having fought the many-headed beast of the lake, he did not like the idea of being pulled apart and shared!

Yet Princess Eleanor seemed admirably relaxed, Thomas thought, considering there were thirteen dragons of *any* size on the island. Her calm helped him to quash his thoughts of getting eaten.

He would stay steady on—he knew how to be stubborn. And Sir Gerald had admonished him to do what needed to be done. He reached into his pocket and touched Isabel's horse. What if it were Isabel who needed rescuing? A line from his oath to the king came to him: . . . *to the end of my days.* "So be it," he whispered.

Eleanor gave him a questioning glance. "What was that?"

He squared his shoulders and stood as straight and steady as he could. "Your Highness, I promised the king I would rescue you. Do you know where I might find these thirteen dragons, that I might confront them and win your release?"

"La!" Eleanor surprised him by giggling. "But of course!" she said, rising from her seat upon the rock.

Thomas scowled, his face flushed. Was she teasing him?

She approached Thomas. "Do not fear that I laugh at you, good knight! I laugh because, in truth, you see before you not a Princess of the Realm, but the nursemaid of Bridgoltha's clutch of twelve dragonlets. Queen Bridgoltha is the last adult dragon hereabouts, so she has had to take human nursemaids to meet her brood's constant demands."

A nursemaid? Twelve of the dragons were babies! That's what she meant when she said twelve were small. Then Thomas wondered, *How small?*

Eleanor was bending to pick up her buckets. "In fact, I must be returning in case Queen Bridgoltha wakens from her sleep."

"Here!" cried Thomas. "Allow me to assist you, Your Highness." He raced forward to retrieve the yoke.

"Thomas," she chided, gently touching his bruised shoulder, "I see you are sore tired from your trials to get here—despite your stout heart that would go into battle against dragons without hesitation!" She waved him away from the yoke and the buckets. "I often helped about the stables when I was younger. I can manage the yoke, and you must come along and allow *me* to care for you until your strength has returned."

She smiled and picked up the sturdy pole with the buckets. "Besides," she added, "the buckets are hanging too long for you. They would drag along the ground and spill out all the fresh water. Come now, don't argue. I shall explain things as we go along." So Thomas, to his chagrin, trotted behind the princess while she led the way to a spring just beyond the beach.

Along the way she told Thomas, "I've given this a great deal of thought, Sir Thomas. Somehow I must leave under agreed-upon terms with the she-dragon."

"Terms?" Thomas wondered how in the world one came to terms with a dragon.

"Terms!" She nodded. "You see, Queen Bridgoltha is from an ancient and respected family. I do not believe she cares overly much for this modern practice of rescuing princesses. An honorable arrangement with agreeable terms on both sides seems to be the best strategy. You know, dragons love a good bargain. They're very competitive

and can't stand to be bested in any activity what-
soever.

"However, I haven't much with which to
bargain. Gold and jewels she does not need. She
does not want land. She loves Barren Isle and only
rarely travels; and those trips have been solely to
get fresh nursemaids.

"Therefore, were I to be rescued, Queen Bridgoltha might bring terror to the good people along
the coast until she had stolen another nursemaid.
I would not bring the fear of losing a daughter or
a wife down upon the heads of my people. Nor
would the king wish me to. The problem is, dragonlets mature very slowly. These will need a
nursemaid for many years yet. So can you understand my dilemma?"

"Yes, my lady." Thomas *did* understand. As
they walked along a well-worn path around the
base of one of the two peaks, he thought about
losing one of his sisters, or Ma, to a dragon.

Eleanor explained that there was an entrance
to the nursery nearby and that she made several
trips a day for water, as the young dragons drank
a great deal. It helped to keep the untrained fires

in their bellies from suddenly erupting and burning their throats. Thomas ran his hand over his
bare chest. Now he wished he had back his old
homespun shirt as well.

Suddenly the princess ducked behind a boulder
and into a dark passageway. "Just through here,"
Eleanor directed as she started forward.

"My lady! My lady!" Thomas whispered.

The princess stopped and turned. "Yes?"

Thomas didn't know how to begin. "Will it
not . . . not seem *unusual* for you to return with
another person? Perhaps I should sneak in?"

"Whatever for?"

"I'll be trespassing into her lair, and . . . and
there's her treasure she'll be guarding. I don't
have any weapon to protect you." Thomas held
out his hands to indicate that he hadn't even
picked up a stick.

"Oh, Thomas." Eleanor stopped in the entry-
way. "I'm afraid I haven't had time to tell you all
you need to know. However, know this: Queen
Bridgoltha sleeps deeply and often. A dragon
needs a lot of rest for at least a hundred years
after laying a clutch of eggs. The dragon queen's

only had about eighty years so far. Whenever she can, she leaves the nursery to me, goes behind a rock wall nearby, and sleeps."

Princess Eleanor put her hand on Thomas's shoulder. "Also, you should know that most of the stories people tell about her are greatly exaggerated. I suspect she does not mind that; it keeps people away from her island. As to her treasure . . ."

Eleanor's voice trailed off, and she gave Thomas a mysterious smile. "It is true she does guard that fiercely. However, it is worth all you have been through just to glimpse it. Very few get to do that.

"Now do not worry about me. Her need protects me from her wrath. I suspect she will not harm you, either." Eleanor paused for a moment and then rushed on. "At least not right away. She does not need to eat much during this time. Besides, she will first want to determine whether you are of any use to her. I've learned that she is a practical queen."

Thomas gulped. He hoped the princess was right.

chapter 21

They descended along the passageway toward the nursery.

Thomas had wanted to place himself in front of the princess to protect her. It was the chivalrous thing to do. But she had refused. "After all," she'd cautioned, "the babies will be expecting me, not you. Also, you don't know the warning signs. If one of them has a tummyache, it could be dangerous." She whispered, "And I want to make sure their mother is asleep before we venture too far in. The little ones may have been naughty in my absence and awakened her."

Thomas smelled the dragon nursery well before

they came to it. The air was full of baby odors, a bit sweet and a little rank—these were smells slightly familiar to him. From somewhere nearby came a steady rhythmic sound, a deep vibrating hum. Thomas could feel it reverberating in the rock all around and rising into his bones. Eleanor nodded, as if she was satisfied about that. When they entered the open nursery, she ran ahead to a large outcropping at the side and peered around it.

Then she backed away and waved Thomas toward a shallow pool in the rock at one side of the cavern. "The dragon queen is sleeping soundly," she told Thomas as he helped her dump the buckets of fresh water into the pool. "That sound is her deep breathing. It takes a loud ruckus or other problem to wake her. As long as you hear that steady thrumming, you shouldn't have to worry."

With the sudden sound of the water splashing on the rocks, a rising chorus of mews and cries came from around the nursery. Out from moss-lined crannies and a grass-filled alcove tumbled the dragonlets. They were each almost as long as

Thomas's arms, and slender. Their heads, when stretched up, did not reach quite to his knees. Their pointed, canine-looking snouts flashed with the small tips of red tongues, and a tiny topknot of downy feathers adorned the head of each.

Thomas caught his breath, and then he let it out in one incredulous sigh. They were the most beautiful things he'd ever seen! Their smooth, iridescent baby scales shimmered, even in the gloom of the cave. Tiny wings glittered—gold and silver—as they unfolded from rippling backs. Their fuzzy topknots fluttered with excitement. Their deeply lidded bronze-colored eyes swept from Eleanor to Thomas and back to the princess. They seemed to be wondering who, or what, this other thing was that walked on two legs.

Several of the dragonlets crowded around the shallow basin to drink. After they had their fill, they came to Eleanor, who was perched on the ledge that surrounded the pool. She scratched under chins and ran her finger down their backs. Her eyes had a faraway, dreamy look. "See their gold and silver wings, and their glinting eyes? This is the dragon's *real* treasure, her children. I think

the old tales of dragons sitting on hoards of treasure were brought back by wanderers who didn't know that they were seeing a mother with her young."

Thomas stood quietly by Eleanor's side. One of the biggest babies had the courage to come down to the floor and nudge Thomas's ankle with his snout. Then he looked up at Thomas as though expecting . . . *what?* Thomas bent over and scratched it along the back of its head, and was surprised to hear a purring sound. He didn't know dragons purred! It was a soft, sweet rumble.

Thomas smiled—but only for a moment. Suddenly there was a splashing tumult in the pool. Two of the dragonlets were wrestling, wrapping their sinewy bodies around each other and rolling over and over in the water. Princess Eleanor jumped up and cried, "Here! Stop that! You'll awaken your mother, and you know how grouchy she can be. You don't want to do that."

Thomas reacted instinctively from his years as a big brother. He leaned over the pool and pulled a dragonlet from the snarling ball with one hand. Then he picked up the second dragonlet with his other hand. He tucked the creatures firmly against his sides. They were wiggly and solid, but no more so than his brothers and sisters were when he had to separate *them*.

"Enough of that," ordered Thomas as loudly as he dared, "or there'll be no special treat tonight for you!"

The two little dragons suddenly stopped wiggling and craned their necks around to look up at him. "He started it," complained the one with bluer scales.

"I did not!" snarled the one with redder scales, jutting his jaw out.

Thomas almost dropped them.

The astonished look on Sir Thomas's face made Eleanor laugh. She put her hand over her mouth to hide her smile. "Aren't they absolutely wonderful?" she said.

chapter 22

"**I**-I didn't know, my lady, I—" Thomas stuttered as he set them both gently down.

"No, I don't suppose many do know they can speak," Eleanor said. "In battle, I doubt that anyone takes the time to sit down and chat with them."

Suddenly a soft question came from behind the princess. "Who's this?"

Eleanor twisted around upon the wide ledge to reveal a much smaller dragon hiding behind her. "Bittany," the princess said, lifting the tiny dragon onto her lap with one hand. "There you are! You don't need to hide. This is Sir Thomas, a friend of mine."

Bittany tucked her sleek crimson head under Eleanor's arm; the rest of her wiggled excitedly in the princess's lap. "Hello," came Bittany's muffled response from her hiding place.

The princess stroked Bittany's back. "She was the last one hatched, and so she's the tiniest. The eggs hatch over the course of several years. However, don't let this shy performance fool you; she is a little terror when she wants to be."

"Me?" asked Bittany, suddenly whipping her head out and looking up at Eleanor.

"Yes, you are, sometimes," the princess answered, and tapped the tip of the dragonlet's nose.

For that bit of good news, Bittany clambered partway up Eleanor's chest with her short front legs and licked the princess under the chin with a dainty tongue.

Thomas smiled and then felt something tugging at his legs. He looked down. The two dragonlets he'd separated were chewing at his breeches.

Thomas pulled the cloth out of their mouths. "Hey!"

Princess Eleanor leaned over and raised a warning finger at them. "Sir Thomas is our guest," she said firmly. "It is not mannerly to chew on the breeches of guests."

Then, to Thomas's surprise, the two dragons lowered themselves and rolled so that their stomachs were exposed.

"They turn belly-up when apologizing," Eleanor explained. "It's as though they are offering their softest spot to be hurt in return, in case they have unwittingly offended." She added, "You need to touch their bellies, or tickle them there, so they know you've accepted their apology."

Thomas knelt down and wonderingly touched their soft underbellies. What a surprise dragons were! The two rolled back up and settled comfortably by his feet.

The princess said, "The larger ones are teething, so they like to chew on soft things. It makes their gums feel better. Still, they need to learn their manners."

"Me have manners," Bittany piped up.

"*I* have manners," Eleanor corrected her.

"Me too!" said Bittany.

The princess laughed and rolled her eyes at Thomas. "You see, Thomas. The young ones need

someone to help with their training. Otherwise, we may have another unwanted dragon war in a hundred years, or less. It can only help to raise a clutch of educated dragons. Their mother, when she wakens for short periods, trains them in fire-breathing, flying, and other dragonly subjects such as dragon history and storytelling. I teach manners, elocution, and courtly subjects like—"

Bittany interrupted. "Tumbleson knows lots of stories! Sometimes I want to climb up, up, up on Mama when he tells a scary one. Only, Nursie said *no* when Mama's sleeping, 'cause Mama gets angry." Bittany looked up at Eleanor.

"That's right," said the princess.

"Tumbleson is that one, there." She pointed out a pale gray dragonlet sitting off to the side. "He was named Tumbleson because immediately after he hatched, he tumbled out of the nest. He's being trained to be the family historian." She smiled at the quiet Tumbleson.

Turning back to Bittany, she added, "But remember, Bittany, we are not supposed to interrupt when someone is speaking."

"Me sorry, Nursie," Bittany said as her topknot quivered. Then she turned so her belly was exposed. Eleanor tickled Bittany's belly, and the tiny dragon righted herself and proceeded to bathe a back leg with her darting tongue.

"They call me Nursie," Eleanor explained.

A dragon from the floor spoke up. "We've had seven nursies, counting this one."

Thomas looked down. Around his feet had gathered the rest of the brood.

Thomas fleetingly wondered what had happened to the other nursies, but did not have time to ask before another dragon said, "Rendall knows how to count."

Yet another chimed in, "I can count to thirteen. One, two—"

"Who wants to hear *you* count?" scoffed a bigger dragonlet.

"Show-off," one of them muttered.

"Dragons!" warned the princess in a low, stern voice. They fell silent. "That's better."

After a moment, Tumbleson nosed forward through his siblings and wobbled a bit as he sat back on his haunches. The dragonlet raised his head high. "May I ask a question, Nursie?"

She nodded. "Yes."

"Our guest said there might be a special treat tonight. We were wondering what it might be." Suddenly twelve sets of eager, glowing eyes fastened on to Thomas.

Thomas licked his lips. He hadn't thought that far ahead; he'd just said what he usually said at home when he had to break up a row. He thought of the bedtime rituals in his home. "Do you like stories?"

"Oh, yes . . . ," came the reply from all of them

at once. There was a chorus of "Tumbleson tells stories!" "Are your stories scary?" "Are you a historian?" "I loooove stories!"

"Shhh!" warned the princess. "Please. One at a time."

A larger dragonlet spoke up. "Do you know a scary story?"

Thomas thought a moment and said, "Scary? Like about fighting drag—" He caught himself and stopped in time when he saw Eleanor shaking her head vigorously. "Oh. Ah . . ." He floundered, trying to think of a suitably scary topic that did not involve dragons. "Um . . ."

"Do you know a story about battling with shiny two-legged men of metal?" asked Tumbleson.

"Carrying long stingers?" added a sibling. "Or men of metal riding atop long-legged beasts with flowing manes and tails?"

"Knights," whispered the princess. "And horses."

"Oh, yes!" said Thomas. "I know those kinds of stories."

"Can you make it not *too* scary?" came one timid voice.

So it was that after the dragonlets had eaten a supper of raw fish from the bay, and he and Princess Eleanor had eaten a delicious meal of cooked fish, Sir Thomas found himself lying on a bed of sweet grasses surrounded by sleepy baby dragons and one tired princess. Thomas yawned and, as promised, told a story of Sir Galahad riding off in shiny armor on a quest to save a damsel locked in a tower.

It was one of his father's favorite stories. Thomas was happy to share it, for as he spoke, he thought of his father and how excited Da would be to hear of the dragons. Thomas told himself he needed to remember every detail about them. Oh, what stories he'd be able to tell when he returned home!

When Thomas finished the story, he heard drowsy grunts, whimpers, and soft snores from the baby dragons and Princess Eleanor. Cradling them all were the humming, deep exhalations of the sleeping dragon mother.

Tumbleson crawled toward Thomas and nuzzled him. He said, "You forgot the ending."

"The ending?" said Thomas. "You mean, *They lived happily ever after*?"

"No." Tumbleson prodded him again. "The dragon ending," he said. *"As was the way, it was done."*

"As was the way, it was done?" asked Thomas.

Tumbleson had curled into a ball and closed his eyes. "Yes," he murmured, and drifted off to sleep.

Thomas stroked Tumbleson's soft topknot of baby feathers and whispered, "As was the way, it was done."

What a fine ending to a tale, thought Thomas. *I'll have to tell Da.*

Thomas made himself comfortable in the soft nest. Then he put his hand in his pocket and brought out the wooden horse. Clutching it close, he shut his tired eyes. Bittany scooted over and curled up behind his knees. She snuggled her tail around his foot, and began to purr.

chapter 23

Thomas awoke when a raspy tongue washed over his face. He found Bittany with her front legs on his chest, staring intently into his face. "Me helped you get awake," she said.

"Bittany, didn't I tell you to let Sir Thomas sleep?" Eleanor walked over, lifted Bittany from Thomas's chest, and set her down in the grassy bed. "He had a difficult journey getting here. We need to treat him gently for a few days," she cautioned.

"I'm fine, my lady," he said to the princess, though he was feeling quite stiff all over. "I slept

well." And he had, to his amazement—sleeping so close to Bridgoltha! He shut his eyes for a moment more and felt the deep hum of the dragon mother's breathing. Good.

When he opened his eyes again, Bittany had rolled over, letting him know she was sorry for waking him. He yawned and sat up to tickle her apologetic belly. Bittany righted herself and asked, "Want to play with your toy beast?"

Thomas was puzzled. "My toy beast?"

Bittany scrabbled around in the sleeping nest and uncovered Isabel's horse.

Thomas picked it up and brushed away some dried bits of grass. It had been played with by Isabel for a couple of years, and Thomas had to admit that it was so scuffed up, it might be mistaken for a beast! "It must have fallen out of my hand during the night," he said. "It's my little sister Isabel's horse. Da carved it."

Bittany asked, "Does your horse-beast help you sleep?"

Thomas nodded. "Yes, it does."

Bittany sniffed it and, leaning close, whispered, "Sister has a rock in the bed. No one's supposed to know!"

Thomas laughed.

"And Rendall's got a stick. Your horse-beast's not scary. Can we play with it?"

Thomas started to say *certainly* when he noticed all the other dragonlets wide-awake and watching from beyond the sleeping area. Did they all want to play with Isabel's horse? He wasn't sure what to say.

Eleanor answered for him, "Perhaps after breakfast. And *only* if Sir Thomas feels strong enough to play. Now, I've brought fresh water for you." There was some halfhearted grumbling, but all the babies filed out into the general nursery area and were soon interested in the pool.

Later, accompanied by the princess and Thomas, they traveled up a wide tunnel that led them beneath a towering overhang and out into the sunlight. On this side of the mountain, the cave's entrance was immense and opened onto a high ledge. They were far above the beach in the distance.

The dragonlets crowded the edge, peering over the straight drop. Thomas kept glancing at them. He was tempted to snatch them away from a possible fall.

"The little ones take flying lessons here," said Eleanor. "You don't need to worry. They are quite safe, but they won't show you their skills. Most of them are only beginning their lessons, so their mother must be here when they fly."

Looking out at the red-pebbled beach, the blue of the bay shaded by wispy white clouds, and the green countryside beyond, Thomas said, "I can see why Queen Bridgoltha loves her island."

Princess Eleanor nodded, scanning the horizon in silence. Then she said, "I love this view as well.

And to see the young ones fly against the golden sunset . . . Oh! It takes my breath away. When I leave, I will miss that."

"Wyndeth can do a loopy-loop," said one dragon sitting by Thomas's foot.

"Can he? I'd love to see that someday," said Thomas.

Then the dragonlets let loose with many tiny snorting puffs of smoke. Thomas's eyes widened. What were they doing now? He glanced toward the princess.

Eleanor was smiling. "They're laughing. Wyndeth is a *she*."

"Oh. I'm . . ." Thomas stopped in the middle of his sentence and studied the group. He saw one yellowish dragon with its head hanging and its topknot limp. It was not snorting. He stepped to its side. "Wyndeth?"

She nodded without raising her head.

Thomas sat down beside her and leaned back on his elbows. "I'm sorry," he said.

Wyndeth looked at him gravely. She laid a foot lightly upon his stomach. Without a shirt, Thomas's chest and stomach were exposed and her small claws were sharp. Thomas felt them pressing on his skin, but she was careful not to hurt him. After a moment she withdrew her foot.

As Eleanor looked down at the scene, her eyes shone. She nodded. "You are *truly* a Knight of the Realm, Sir Thomas." Then, with a little laugh, she added, "And we must do something about your attire. A Knight of the Realm should not go about half-dressed. Though, I must admit, you are fresher-smelling than the first time we met."

Thomas blushed, remembering his and Jon's slide through Heartwind's stall.

The princess continued, "I think I can find something that might fit you from one of the previous nurses. There are a few bits and pieces stowed away in one of the smaller caves."

Thomas played with the dragons, scooting pebbles off the ledge. He instructed them in sharing. They each got a turn to nose Isabel's wooden horse-beast past a line Thomas had scraped on the ledge.

A few of the smaller dragons were growing grouchy. "Time for naps!" called Eleanor. One or two of the bigger dragonlets complained under their breath, but they prodded the sleepier ones along as they all trundled back into the nursery. Thomas carried a dozing Bittany. Her tiny claws gripped Isabel's horse close to her chest.

Inside, Thomas was in charge of getting the babies into one heap while the princess went in search of a shirt for him. Settling the dragonlets wasn't easy, but Thomas had plenty of experience getting young ones to lie down for a nap.

"You!" He pointed to a purple dragon trying to look innocent. "Keep your wings to yourself; stop poking everyone. Fold them up. This is naptime, not playtime." Then he grabbed a silvery dragon and, lifting it into the air, admonished, "It's not polite to chew on your sister's tail. Stop it this instant." When Thomas set the silver one down, the dragonlet showed his belly and apologized to his sister.

By the time Eleanor returned, Thomas had all the dragonlets napping—or, at least, resting and not disturbing those around them. Also, he had managed to pry Isabel's horse out of Bittany's grasp and return it to his pocket. He tried on the short shirt the princess brought him and found it fit very well, although it had a bit more embroidery on it than he might have liked.

"I'm afraid it's a piece of ladies' clothing," Eleanor said. "Do you mind?"

Sir Thomas had been taught to take all gifts graciously, and it *did* fit well. "It is a perfect fit, my lady. Thank you." He bowed.

"We do not need to stand on such high formality here, Thomas."

"Thank you," he said again, simply. Then he asked the question that had been on his mind. "Princess, what happened to the other nursemaids?"

Eleanor smiled. "Has that been worrying you? Two or three were found to be unsuitable and were dropped off again with a warning not to speak of this place. I'm sure they've kept their peace! One does not lightly break a promise to Queen Bridgoltha. One was old and sickly, and Bridgoltha cared for her until she died. And a couple of them . . . well, to be perfectly truthful, I haven't asked about them."

"Oh!" Thomas's face paled for a moment. Then

he added reassuringly, "You *are* very patient with the babies."

Eleanor laid a hand on Thomas's shoulder. "I have done some nursing before, in the stables, and, when I have been needed, on the battlefield. I am not overly worried about my place here. And you have been a great help today. I deeply appreciate it."

"I, too, have done a share of nursing," Thomas replied. "I'm the eldest and now have nine brothers and sisters."

"Ten children in your family! Oh, my . . . often I have wished for just one other, a brother or a sister. It was not to be."

The princess fell quiet for a moment, and then shook her head as though clearing her mind of sad memories. "Forgive me," she said. "I nursed my mother the queen, you see, until she died. And I was thinking about Father. I do hope he gets back safely to the castle. He is all the family I have . . . except for . . ." Her hand swept before her, indicating the sleeping young dragons.

"I'm sure he will," said Thomas. "Jon and Bartholomew will see to that."

Eleanor nodded. "When I was young, I got to raise a number of the pets around the castle. I loved feeding carrots to the donkeys." She laughed a little. "I was forever getting caught with a kitten or a piglet up in my room. I think I frightened a number of tutors away until I was old enough to study on my own. Then I studied with a puppy or a chick on my lap! La! I missed all that once I had to start behaving like a royal lady. Still, my father taught me much. I know I will one day be grateful for his care about my education when I must rule in his stead. I hope that day is yet far away."

She couldn't stop herself from yawning. "Excuse me! I'm afraid that taking care of so many young dragons can wear upon a person." She chuckled. "I understand why there have been six nursemaids before me!"

She hid another yawn with her hand and said, "Thomas, you once placed yourself at my service. If I may, I will put you to that task now. The babies will sleep for a good while. If you do not mind staying here with them, I thought I might go back to the ledge and rest in the sun. I rarely get to be by myself these days. You can hear that their mother is still sleeping, and I looked in at her as I came back with that shirt. I'm sure you'll be quite safe. Feel free to take a nap with the little ones if you wish."

Thomas did not particularly like the idea of Princess Eleanor's leaving him with Bridgoltha so close—even if he could hear the she-dragon sleeping. How would he explain himself without the princess's help should the dragon queen awaken? However, it was obvious that Eleanor was exhausted being the nursemaid to so many, and he had learned that a knight is always gallant to a lady. "Please," he told her, "you *must* rest. Go sit in the sun. I shall stay here and watch over them."

Book VI

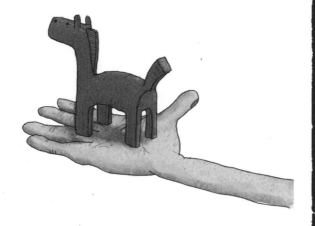

of Toys and Talents

chapter 24

Thomas resisted the urge to peek at the dragon queen. He could hear her deep breathing, and he didn't want to do anything that might suddenly waken her. He settled down upon the floor near the sleeping area, and leaned back against the rock wall. He stretched his legs out into the open cavern, crossed his ankles, put his hand in his pocket, and withdrew Isabel's horse. He stared at it for a moment with tired eyes before he smiled and put it back in his pocket. His eyes shut—*for just a moment,* he thought. He was still so weary from wrestling the beast in the lake and freeing the young dolphin. He needed a nap, too.

Sir Thomas slept so deeply that it was only with a sudden start that he awoke and realized something was wrong. A horrible wailing sounded nearby. He shook his head to clear it, and looked toward the babies. Bittany was out of the sleeping nest and sprawled upon the hard floor of the open nursery.

She was panting, her topknot drooped, and her scales glistened with sweat. Every few moments she wobbled her head upright and wailed cries that were scratchy and so loud that Thomas feared his eardrums would burst. The pain she seemed to be in pierced Thomas all the way to his heart. It was kicking so hard in his chest, it hurt.

It was important not to panic. For a moment Thomas wondered if he should fetch Princess Eleanor from the ledge. He wasn't sure what to do, but his heart told him to stay and comfort the distressed baby as he would have Isabel, or any of his other siblings. He needed to find out what was happening. "Bittany," he said, kneeling before her and touching her lightly, "what's wrong? Where does it hurt, little one? Can you tell me?"

Bittany lifted her head limply and stared at him with watery eyes. She wailed again and rolled awkwardly; her short legs jerked in the air. Thomas moved to her side and began to inspect her. Her tummy was bulging, and she felt feverish. There wasn't the usual coolness of dragon scales Thomas had already grown used to.

He knew about fevers. Everyone in his family had had them at one time or another. They were dangerous. The first thing to do was to cool the person as quickly as possible. Perhaps it was the same with dragons?

He ran to the pool. Taking off the shirt he wore, he dipped it in the cold water. "Not little Bittany!" he muttered as he wrung out some of the water and ran back to her. He wiped her sides gently with the wet cloth. She wailed. He whispered to her all the while, "This will make you feel better. There . . . there . . ."

Suddenly a thunderous voice boomed, "Stand back!"

Thomas jerked, tumbling backward. He let go of Bittany—just as she burped a flame of red-hot fire. It shot straight upward. Thomas's face would have been in that flame if he hadn't been warned!

He blinked. The flame had pierced the gloom of the nursery and blinded him for a moment with its brightness. He got to his knees and rubbed his eyes. When he could see again, he searched the floor for Bittany. She seemed to be better. She was on her feet and toddling quickly toward . . . toward . . . Thomas gulped. She was headed toward a set of immense talons. Each claw was as long as one of Thomas's legs!

His eyes climbed higher and higher—past the arched yellow claws, along the streaked and scarred scales covering a gigantic muscular body, up and up, until he was looking at the grimacing face of a huge dragon. Its head stretched up into the dark reaches of the high nursery cavern. Thomas sprawled backward.

"Mama!" cried Bittany, climbing onto a huge foot. "Me burped."

"And a good one it was," commented the dusky voice in a softer tone. Then the dragon's head moved lower as though to get a better look at Thomas. Queen Bridgoltha moved her head slowly one way and then another, looking at him with each eye in turn. Finally, she leaned in and sniffed at him. Her tremendous topknot of brightly colored feathers swooshed past Thomas.

It felt as if she were inhaling all the air from the cave. Thomas coughed and clung to the rocky floor.

The dragon asked her daughter, "Who is your little friend?"

"Sir Thomas," said Bittany. "He's Nursie's friend. He has a sister called Isabel."

"Sir?" questioned Queen Bridgoltha, raising her voice again.

Thomas covered his ears. Bittany jumped off her mother's feet and scrambled toward her brothers and sisters, who were all awake and huddled wary-eyed.

A huge cloud of smoke and snorting laughter filled the chamber. The queen slapped her tail on the floor. It seemed to shake the whole mountain. Then she lowered herself as though she were settling in for a friendly visit. Her head was closer to Thomas now. She asked him, in a slightly hissing manner, "Sssir? Surely you are not a knight. Thomas, was it?"

Thomas nodded. He had not found his voice yet. But from behind him he heard a soft "Your Majesty!" He peeked over his shoulder quickly to see Princess Eleanor bowing at the entrance to the nursery.

The dragon queen seemed satisfied that her nursemaid was here as well. "Enter!" she commanded. Then she refolded her front legs under her, and as she did so, her talons screeched across the floor, producing lines of flame. That seemed to please her—she flicked the tip of a gigantic tongue across her face.

Eleanor helped Sir Thomas to his feet. She shot him a warning glance and whispered, "Do not try to trick her. Bridgoltha can smell trickery." Thomas nodded slightly. The two of them stood before the dragon queen.

Queen Bridgoltha studied Thomas without any hurry. Finally, she turned her attention to Eleanor. "Nursie, you left my children with this stranger?"

"Your Majesty," Eleanor replied, "Thomas is a noble Knight of the Realm. He would never harm your children. He has a good deal of experience with young ones, and is quite charmed by yours."

The dragon queen considered this a moment and said, "I saw that he has won the affection of Bittany. However, we both know that is not difficult to do. Even if this *unkempt* example of your kind is truly a Knight of the Realm, it makes no difference. It is *I* who make decisions about my children. Henceforth, please remember that! Now, Nursie, take your charges in hand. I'm afraid I was startled out of my sleep by my daughter's cries, and"—the dragon paused to rest her head lightly upon an upraised knee, her great jaws moving closer to Thomas—"I am *not* in the best of moods at the moment."

chapter 25

Thomas finally managed to swallow, and Eleanor did as Bridgoltha had instructed. She moved to sit with the dragonlets crowded around her. They watched fearfully from the nursery's nest while Thomas faced their mother alone.

Sir Thomas stiffened his leg muscles and willed himself to stay upright. If it came to it, he would meet his doom, and the end of his quest, standing up like a knight. He owed that to his parents, to his king, and to Princess Eleanor for their faith in him.

The very fact that he wasn't eaten already served to give him some hope. Perhaps, as the princess had said, the dragon queen might determine that he could be of use to her. He prayed so. Then he could work out a way to rescue Princess Eleanor.

Thomas sensed that Queen Bridgoltha's temper was running high but she was controlling it. Her voice was softer now—this only made it sound deadlier.

"Let's get acquainted, Thomas, shall we? Would you like to sit?"

Thomas found his voice at last. "Thank you, no. I . . . I prefer to stand, if you don't mind, my . . ." He'd started to say *my lady* and realized that might not be correct; it might even be insulting. How did one address a queen dragon? He bowed and finished by calling her "Your Majesty," as Princess Eleanor had done.

Queen Bridgoltha nodded slightly, and Thomas felt her hot breath sweep across his bare chest. "As you wish," she said, and added, "You have been raised with manners. I appreciate that. So often one simply hears screams and then must dodge the rudest of personal affronts as weapons of all sorts are sent hurtling onward. That sort of behavior is really not conducive to civilized conversation, is it?"

Sir Thomas raised his head to address her. "I suppose not, Your Majesty."

The dragon queen was silent for a moment. Then she said, "Thomas, you are particularly small, I believe, even for a knight. You are young. Is that not so?"

"You are correct." Thomas looked down at himself. His footwear was scruffy, his breeches were ragged. He still bore many scabs, scratches, and purple bruises from his battle at the lake. He could see why she had referred to him as unkempt. He was sure he did not strike anyone who looked at him as a knight. But there was absolutely nothing he could do about his size. He added, "There are some things about oneself that must simply be accepted and worked around."

The queen's huge eyes widened at that. "Well said, *Sir* Thomas."

Thomas swallowed again and felt his shakes start to subside. She had called him *sir*. It was a slight victory, but only momentarily felt—for the next thing she said frightened Thomas anew.

"So we understand each other. After all, there are things about dragons that must simply be accepted. For example, we *do* eat meat, wandering loiterers, errant knights . . . that sort of thing." She cooed the words, not taking her eyes off Thomas.

Thomas blanched but held his ground. There was no use trying to run; she had turned her immense body to block both tunnels to the outside. In addition, he did not wish to do anything rash that would direct her wrath toward Princess Eleanor for allowing him into the nursery. He braced himself for the attack. . . .

It did not come. When he could breathe a little easier, he met Bridgoltha's stare. Thomas saw puzzlement there in the sparking depths of her eyes, and something else . . . amusement? He wasn't sure. Had she just been baiting him? If it was amusement—it prickled at the edge of his control. He did not mind being eaten in one gulp. However, he minded very much being toyed with in front of others he cared for, like Princess Eleanor and the babies. It wasn't right to make fun of someone—especially if you meant

to hurt them. It was like a cat playing with its food before killing and eating it. He wouldn't have any of it!

Abruptly, he knelt on one knee and bowed his head. With dignity, he said, "Please eat me now if you are going to, Your Majesty."

A puff of smoke filled the nursery and Thomas heard a loud snort. Queen Bridgoltha was laughing! Thomas clenched his fists, almost ready *to demand* that she eat him. How *dare* she? He shook—not with fear but with anger. He'd offered his life . . . and she had laughed at him!

Thomas fumbled a bit at his side until he remembered that he no longer carried Starfast. To Queen Bridgoltha, he *was* something small and pathetic—something to be laughed at. He squeezed his eyes shut for a moment. How silly to demand to be eaten! That would certainly have ended the quest in a hurry. Had he learned nothing at all?

With the realization of how foolish he was being, Sir Gerald's words came back to him. He must not let his anger get in the way of what he needed to do. He suddenly pictured the brave squire he'd seen at his first battle. He had resolutely, and quietly, taken the place of his fallen knight. Thomas breathed deeply, rose to his feet, and squared his shoulders. He, too, would do his duty. The princess, and the kingdom, still needed him. He waited before the queen of the dragons.

"Let's not be so hasty, my brave young knight," the queen said. "Yes. You amuse me, and I can see you are affronted at that. But do not take my amusement as belittling to you. You have roused my curiosity, so let's have no more of this *gobble-me-up* foolishness. If anything, let's say I was simply testing your resolve."

Thomas searched her eyes. Had he passed her test?

Bridgoltha tilted her head toward him; her colorful topknot brushed the side of the cavern. "Now, Sir Thomas . . ." She nodded—slightly—as though honoring his knighthood, and continued, "A knight this far from home must be on a quest. Yours is?"

"To rescue Princess Eleanor, your nursie."

"Ahh!" Thomas was almost knocked back by the force of her breath as she voiced that syllable.

"I thought a champion might attempt the rescue of someone so highly born as our new nursemaid. However, it was a risk I took to secure a nursie who might instill some courtly manners in my unpolished brood. A mother wants only the best for her young. I'm sure you understand."

Thomas nodded.

The queen continued, "Since there are so few dragons about these days due to . . . let us be frank, the interference of two-legged warriors, such as knights . . . I've been forced to turn to your kind for our nursies."

Now a bright glint flared in the dragon's eyes. She paused for a moment before asking, "Was there more to your quest? What were you to do if you met with *resistance,* for example?"

"I'm to rescue the princess, and . . . and . . ."

"And? Out with it!" snapped Bridgoltha. "Were you to kill me?"

From the sleeping nest, Thomas heard the sound of a dozen baby dragons gasping all at once. Quickly, he said, "Only if it was necessary, Your Majesty."

Queen Bridgoltha closed her eyes, raised her

head, and breathed angry red flames up into the dark recesses of the cavern roof.

For an instant, Thomas saw scorch marks on the smooth underside of the rock far above him. He knew she would eventually turn her baleful eyes upon him again.

chapter 26

She did turn to eye him again, but it was not with the intention of frying him in flames—at least not yet. Instead, she seemed to have gotten rid of some of her pent-up anger.

She propped her chin upon one leathery foot and said quite calmly, "How unimaginative! Really, is your kind always so boring? Kill this, kill that, if it gets in your way. . . . How narrow-minded. At least you, Sir Thomas, are delightfully honest about it." Then she raised her head again and looked around the nursery. "I suppose you have all your knightly equipment stowed hereabouts— your iron stinger-blade with a fancy name?"

Thomas shook his head. "No. I had a sword

named Starfast. . . ." He paused. "But it was broken and lost in the lake across the bay."

"Hmm! Clumsy of you. However, I certainly sympathize. We dragons do not like the look and smell of that lake, either. Well then, where is your loyal mount? Your warhorse? Does it await you across the bay?"

"No, Your Majesty." Thomas shook his head again. "I had one, a donkey named Bartholomew. But I loaned him to another who needed assistance."

"A donkey! Hah!" She snorted and more smoke floated up to the ceiling. "A generous deed, but a foolish act on your part, I think. One never knows when a fast and fearless . . . well, a *steady* steed might come in handy, such as when running away from dragons. So-o-o . . . ." She tapped her chin with a glass-hard claw. "I see you do not wear a silver shirt of metal, or a padded vest, to protect you from an easy roasting."

Thomas touched his bare skin. "No. I had a leather jerkin, but it was stolen from me by dolphins."

At this the queen chuckled, and a number of small misty clouds drifted upward. "My, my,

Thomas, you let your guard down. How gullible of you! Everyone knows that the dolphins of this sea are playful little thieves. We'll probably find your jerkin tossed out upon the beach one day. It's their way of saying, 'Your turn!' "

The queen laughed again. "Now, let me see if I have heard all this correctly." As she spoke, she ticked off each item on a hooked yellow claw. "You lost your sword. You loaned your steed. You allowed your jerkin to be stolen. So that makes you clumsy, foolish, *and* gullible." She sighed, a deep dragonly whoosh that swept through the room.

For some strange reason, that deep sigh calmed Thomas. She was right, of course, about his faults. *What a champion I've made,* he thought as he stared at his feet. He was certainly a sorry excuse for a knight!

Queen Bridgoltha asked, "Thomas, tell me, are these the qualities that become a knight nowadays?"

Thomas did not look up. He shook his head. "No."

"Have you any weapon or equipment at all for your quest?"

Thomas spread his arms outward. "Alas, no, Your Majesty."

It was absolutely quiet in the nursery. Even the babies had stilled their whining and had stopped fighting over Princess Eleanor's lap—which was the best seat for viewing all that was happening.

It was Thomas who broke the silence. He finally raised his head. With his hands and fingers spread wide, he looked deep into Bridgoltha's bronze eyes and said, "I have nothing."

"Well," said the queen, "I must say this is refreshing! For a change, a would-be champion comes equipped just as we dragons always are . . . empty-handed. How absolutely delicious! We face each other with nothing but our natural talents. *Ooooh*, let me think about how we should proceed." Queen Bridgoltha laid her chin down upon an outstretched foot.

It was precisely at this crucial moment that Bittany decided to speak with her mother. She slithered off Nursie's lap, and before Eleanor could retrieve her, she marched up to her mother's chin.

"Mama?"

The queen rolled her eyes downward toward her daughter. She started to reprimand Bittany but had barely begun before Bittany announced, "He *does* have something! It's a horse-beast! It's called a toy. Da made it for Isabel. We played with it."

Queen Bridgoltha looked over at Thomas. "You came armed with *a toy*?"

"Your Majesty, I almost forgot I had it!" Thomas said. He took it from his pocket and held it out for the dragon queen to see.

Bridgoltha stretched out a single claw and lifted it from his hands. She twirled it about for a moment.

Thomas gulped. Was she going to crush it?

Instead, she glanced down at Bittany and said, "You interrupted while Sir Thomas and I were speaking."

Bittany showed her belly to her mother. Gently her mother laid a single claw tip upon it.

Bridgoltha had just turned her attention back to Thomas when Bittany scuttled forward and showed her belly to him. Instantly, the mother dragon's eyebrows rose threateningly, her topknot stiffened, and a rumble began to rise from deep in her throat. She glared at Thomas. But Thomas, who was used to Bittany's ways, knelt quickly and tickled the small dragon—accepting her apology so that she could go back to the others, where it was safe.

The dragon queen made a sound in her throat like a great *harrumph!* She watched her daughter return to the group. She looked back at Thomas and laid Isabel's carved horse on the floor before her. To pick it up, Thomas would have to approach within inches of her wide mouth.

Thomas stared at the small horse. It was all he had left of the gifts given him. And Da had made it! He stepped forward and, bending low before that set of sharp teeth, he picked it up.

chapter 27

The dragon queen raised her heavy lower eyelids partway over her eyes and stared at Sir Thomas through the slits. She did not take her eyes off him as he ran his hands lightly over the toy, smiled to himself, and strode purposefully toward the dragonlets. The small knight knelt down and offered the wooden toy to Bittany.

"When I left home," he said to Bittany, "my sister Isabel gave me this horse. She shared it so that I would not be lonely upon my quest. Now I give it to you. You must learn to share it with your brothers and sisters."

"Take turns?" Bittany asked, her topknot quivering happily.

"Yes. Like when we played with it on the ledge."

Bittany grasped the toy with her tiny claws. She stretched up and licked Thomas along the back of his hand.

When he arose, he walked back to stand before the dragon queen. He took a deep breath and said, "Now I truly have nothing. I stand before you simply as myself. I'm sorry I thought to do you harm, Your Majesty. That was not befitting a knight." Then, slowly but deliberately, he lay down upon the rock floor before her and offered his bare stomach.

Eleanor gasped. The little ones stood at attention—their cries hushed, their topknots alert, and their eyes wide.

If Queen Bridgoltha was surprised, she did not show it. Instead, she raised a claw and licked it. She took her time eyeing this unlikely knight at her feet. She held her claw over his vulnerable stomach. With one swipe she could have split him in two. In a deep voice she said, "You've lied to me, Sir Thomas. Oh, you came here armed with plenty of weapons! You did not lose them on the journey. I see that now."

Thomas closed his eyes. He hadn't lied! He couldn't help it if she didn't believe him. Regardless, he knew in his heart that he owed her this apology.

The last line of his oath to the king came to him. He whispered it to himself: ". . . to the end of my days."

The queen set a curved claw tip lightly upon Sir Thomas's stomach. The tip scratched his skin; it made a bright red line across his middle. In the nest area, Bittany began to whimper and hid her head under Nursie's arm.

Then, gently, Queen Bridgoltha continued, "You came here to *best* me with your bravery and your honesty. You *will not*." The dragon queen raised her claw.

Thomas opened his eyes.

Queen Bridgoltha dipped her head to him. "Your bravery and your honesty are talents that have served you well. Never let it be heard

that one young, ragged knight bested the queen of the dragons in courtly manners! My natural gifts are just as strong as yours. I accept your apology. Rise, Sir Thomas, a Knight of the Realm."

chapter 28

After Sir Thomas's apology there were several days of courtly negotiations to work through. However, the hard work of coming to terms was considerably easier when Queen Bridgoltha and Sir Thomas spoke of the beast in the lake.

"You are quite sure the creature died?" Bridgoltha asked.

"I believe so," said Thomas. "Its tentacles were limp and strewn about the lakeshore."

"Hmm." The dragon queen pondered this. "Dragon lore tells us that the beast was awaiting the return of something a great fish took from it.

That must have been its tooth, the ivory from which your sword's hilt was carved. We dragons have never liked what was living in that lake. But it did serve a purpose in keeping nosy people and fishermen away from my island. Now I suppose I shall need to learn to get along with human neighbors again." She sighed and added, "However, I am impressed by your bravery, my young knight! Now let us see if we are both brave enough, and humble enough, to come to some agreeable terms for our mutual benefit."

The terms agreed upon were that Sir Thomas, Princess Eleanor, and Queen Bridgoltha would take turns caring for the young dragons. This was a solution proposed by Bittany, who insisted that they must all learn how to share.

Sir Thomas would spend one season every year teaching the dragonlets chivalry, sharing, and storytelling, while Eleanor would come one season a year to teach courtly manners, politics, and elocution. Their mother could sleep soundly at those times. She would take care of them the other two seasons with the help of the first-hatched youngsters, who were getting big enough now to take on such chores as fetching water. During this period Wyndeth, the eldest dragonlet, would teach flying lessons, Rendall would teach mathematics, Tumbleson would pass on dragon history to his siblings, and the queen would continue with fire-breathing instruction and the fine art of listening. If these arrangements proved successful, Bridgoltha would not make off with any more nursemaids.

As a favor, Thomas would bring Da to Barren Isle so that she might meet the man who had carved the wonderful horse-beast. In return, she would allow a couple of her dragonlets to visit Thomas in the countryside one day, when they were a little older. This was so that Ma and the others might get a glimpse of some astonishing dragon treasure—her babies.

So it came to pass that on a sunny morning after negotiations had been concluded, Queen Bridgoltha scooped up Sir Thomas and Princess Eleanor and flew them across the bay, around the now peaceful lake, and to the abandoned cottage nearby. She would not take them closer to home at this time, for fear of knights who relied more

upon their man-made weapons than upon their personal talents.

When they alighted on the trail, she bid them farewell. Then the dragon queen said, "There is one more apology that must be made."

Eleanor and Thomas looked puzzled.

"I," said Queen Bridgoltha, "owe Nursie an apology for taking her away from her father and her kingdom, even if I do believe she enjoyed some of her stay with my family." Then Queen Bridgoltha knelt upon the ground and turned toward Princess Eleanor in apology.

Eleanor laid her hand upon the dragon's soft underbelly. "Your gracious apology, great queen, is accepted—upon one condition."

The dragon queen's topknot quivered, and she looked questioningly at Eleanor.

"One day, you must invite my father to see the young ones fly at sunset," Eleanor said. "He would like that."

Queen Bridgoltha nodded. "Of course. My little ones will miss you until your return. And you, Sir Thomas. I hope the food and the clothing we have gathered for you will suffice for your journey home. Travel well."

Sir Thomas and Princess Eleanor walked all that day until they arrived at the cottage of the widow who had fed Thomas so well on his trip to Barren Isle. Again the widow made a humble but tasty meal for the travelers. As she cooked, she recounted the arrival of Bartholomew with the injured king and Jon.

She had cared for the king while Jon had helped with the chores and tended to her animals. It was two days before the king was fit enough to be moved in a neighbor's wagon. They had tied the donkey to the cart, and the king was able to lie down as he rode the rest of the way to the castle.

The next morning that same neighbor left his farm to carry Thomas and Princess Eleanor home. As they traveled, the story of their adventures raced before them faster than wispy clouds on a happy day.

The hill folk in the surrounding countryside came out to cheer the wagon when it passed. And when the farmer, Thomas, and the princess stopped for a meal, people gathered around to touch Thomas for good luck or to slap him on the back for a job well done. A few even said that they might go to the coast to fish again, now that the beast of the lake was dead and the dragons were no longer snatching nursemaids. In fact, several families were planning to visit the once dismal lake, for it was said that the waters had cleared to a shimmering blue after the monster died. And the new, soft grass along its shores made the pool inviting again.

Early one day, while they were coming down from the highlands, Thomas spotted a lone rider on a black horse. It was Sir Gerald; he'd ridden out to meet them.

Dismounting, Sir Gerald gripped Eclipse by the reins and bowed first to Princess Eleanor. "Your Highness," he said. Then, turning to the elderly farmer, he dipped his head and said, "Good sir, you have once again come to the aid of the kingdom. We thank you from our hearts. You will be rewarded well." Lastly, he bowed to Thomas. "Sir Thomas."

Thomas felt uncomfortable when Sir Gerald bowed to him. He clambered quickly down from the wagon seat and gave Sir Gerald a hug. "Sir Gerald," he cried, "you won't believe everything that's happened!"

"Oh, but I would," said Sir Gerald with a laugh. "Stories of your deeds fly before you like the wind. I heard about you as I was coming home from the border."

"Are the northern borders secure yet?" asked the princess.

"For the moment, Your Highness," Sir Gerald replied. "The breach has been repaired, and there are sentries posted to watch for a new uprising from the north."

Eleanor smiled. "That is good," she said. "And my father? We've heard on our travels that he is mending."

"The king is stiff, and just last night was able to walk a bit with a cane. But in all other respects he seems to be healing, my lady. He was, as I left him, peppering the kitchen staff with details for a grand reception in honor of your return and to celebrate our good knight's deeds." Sir Gerald nodded toward Thomas.

"A reception?" asked Thomas.

"A feast," explained Sir Gerald. "And then a ball where you can put to use one of your other talents, your dancing ability. It is gossiped that several ladies of the court are vying for the honor of dancing with you."

"With me? In public?" squeaked Thomas.

"They shall have to wait until I have had my turn," said the princess.

Thomas felt his face grow hot. He hid his blush by turning to Eclipse. "How are you, boy?" he asked the warhorse as he stroked Eclipse's neck.

"He is doing well," put in Sir Gerald, "due to the kind of handling of our newest grooms-man."

"Jon?" asked Thomas.

Sir Gerald nodded. He added, "Jon was ele-vated in rank by Marshal Wattley. Wattley's a cautious man and not given to doling out praise. Still, I think he was so surprised by our young Jon's bravery and hard work that he brought him up from the rather lowly position of an assistant under-groomsman, or some such thing, to just plain groomsman. Apparently, this happened even though—as Marshal Wattley put it—*he is like Sir Thomas, small for his age.*"

"Small for his age?" Thomas said with a splut-ter, and added, "Jon's not—" Then he started laughing and coughing at the same time and could not finish what he'd meant to say.

Soon they were all laughing.

"In truth, I suspect our Wattley is not blind. I think he may have just taken a liking to the young rapscallion," said Sir Gerald. "Come, I will escort you the rest of the way to the castle, where the king, Jon, and Thomas's family are anxiously awaiting your return."

With that, the cart fell in behind Sir Gerald and they continued through the last hours of their journey home. Along the way more and more people came out to join the welcoming crowds.

Thomas saw his family in the throng at the castle gate. Da had Isabel held high in his arms, and Ma was holding the new baby. Peter, who looked as if he'd been recently scrubbed raw, sat atop Albert's broad shoulders. Around them ranged his other brothers and sisters. They were all waving, even Albert.

Thomas stood in the wagon and returned their waves as the cart clattered beneath the raised portcullis and onto the cobblestoned courtyard.

In the great hall, Princess Eleanor ran through the courtiers, knights, and ladies to throw herself into her father's arms. Thomas knew her tears were tears of happiness.

Thomas waited at the back of the room. In the crowd he spied several of the younger knights who had been pages and squires with him. Standing to one side was the brave knight who'd gone into the fight at the pass, when he'd still been a squire. Thomas smiled at him. He was glad that the young man had come home safely from the border.

Sir Edwin was there, too, smoothing his finely embroidered tunic and snickering to a small crowd gathered around him. During their training he'd taken every opportunity to make fun of Thomas. Now, he pointed at Thomas.

Thomas glanced down at the hodgepodge of his clothing. At least he'd been able to replace the shirt the princess had found for him in the nursery. He pulled up on his breeches, raised his eyes, and made a point of smiling at Edwin until the older boy had to look away.

Finally, Thomas was motioned forward by Sir Gerald.

When Thomas approached the king, he knelt on one knee.

"Ah!" said the princess, freeing herself from her father's embrace and wiping her eyes with a piece of lace handed to her by one of the ladies of the court. "Father," she said, "may I present my champion."

Thomas looked up. The entire court, other than Edwin and his friends, were cheering. He blushed. Then he searched the crowd and saw Da.

Da raised his hand and placed it over his heart.

Thomas understood. Da was telling him that his heart and his hand had been strong enough, though he was but the son of a rough leather-smith. Thomas smiled at Da.

He was quickly drawn back to the king who boomed, "Well met again, Sir Thomas!" The king motioned for Thomas to rise. "Thomas, we are greatly in your debt. I believe many a knight twice your size could not have accomplished so much. You defeated the beast of the lake, befriended the queen of the dragons, and rescued my daughter. For such a champion, no reward is too great. How shall I repay you?"

Thomas thought for a moment. He'd only done what he'd felt was the right thing to do. Shoving

Starfast into one of the mouths of the beast had been his only possible course of action at the time. And it was sensible to entrust the king to Jon's care and Bartholomew's steady gait. And apologizing to Queen Bridgoltha had been the proper thing to do—as Ma might have said. Surely he did not need to be rewarded for doing as any clearheaded person might. Then an idea came to him.

"My liege . . ." He hesitated.

"Yes, Thomas?" prompted the king.

"If—if I might be trusted with another sword, I'd like that."

The king laughed. "I think we can see to that. Anything else, Thomas?"

"Well . . ." Thomas licked his lips, not sure if what he was about to say would raise the king's anger. He was not certain how one turned down an invitation by the king, or even if it was something that was allowed. "If—if Your Majesty does not object, I'd like to go with Jon and visit Bartholomew and be excused from the dancing, Sire. That is, if I may."

Everyone in the room seemed to draw in their breath. Then, just as comments began to fly through the crowd, the king threw back his head and laughed heartily. Finally, he said, "Few turn down an invitation by the king. However, you have done me a service beyond measure, Sir Thomas. Fulfilling this simple request is not nearly the reward due you. Still, it is granted. First we will feast. Your parents will be seated in a place of honor. After we have eaten and drunk to your health, you have my leave to go to the stables to visit your friends. You will be excused from the dancing."

Thomas thought he heard a sigh from the ladies in the audience.

Then the king turned to the gathering and said in a louder tone, "Sir Thomas, while you are there, I charge you with ensuring that my apples and pears are not making their way into the bellies of others." He turned back to Thomas, winked, and lowered his voice to add, "Except for one or two to Bartholomew. You understand."

Jon was not at the feast. Afterward, Thomas ran to the stables. He carried a bowl of meat and veg-etables that Dilley, the kitchen maid, had put together for Jon. In his pocket was a newly picked apple for Bartholomew.

When he reached the stables, Thomas found that Bartholomew had been moved from his old, cramped pen to the large stall that had been Heartwind's. It was the stall that had for generations been reserved for the king's favorite.

Jon hugged Thomas and crowed when he saw the dish. He pulled a warm piece of mutton out of the bowl and said, "I didn't go to the hall to eat for fear I'd be made to attend the dance. You won't catch me dipping and strutting about like my trousers are full of fleas."

Thomas laughed. Then he fed the apple to his old traveling companion—patting the donkey and stroking his muzzle. Finally he turned to Jon and pushed him playfully on the shoulder. "What's this about Marshal Wattley thinking you're old enough to be a groomsman? Or that you're just small for your age?"

"S-h-h-h!" cautioned Jon, looking around. "You may be the champion around here, but me? I'm conspiring to become the marshal of these stables one day. Wait and see if I don't!"

Thomas smiled at his friend and then yelled, "Race you!"

Jon dropped the bowl, and they were off.

Late in the deep autumn, when the hills were awash with leaves colored in velvety maroons and brilliant yellows, the elderly king and his daughter traveled through the countryside with a company that included several knights, Jon and some other groomsmen, and Sir Thomas and his family. They visited a kind widow at a humble cottage, and they erected a stone monument to friends beside a shimmering pool.

Moreover, they raised a pavilion on the shore of a bay. Across the water, near the tip of a long causeway, lay the home of the dragons. The king had come to pay his respects to the dragon queen. Princess Eleanor had come to stay for the winter and to teach courtly manners, politics, and elocution.

That evening, just as a last thin line of gold from the sun rimmed the purple twilight, two dragonlets lifted their wings and rose into the sky over the peaks on Barren Isle. More young dragons followed these two. They drifted and turned lazy circles on the last thermals of the day.

In the pavilion, the king and the princess, Sir Gerald, Thomas and his family, Jon, and the rest of the company watched—mouths open with wonder. Isabel stood on her toes, stretched her hands up, and said, "I want to fly, too!"

In the years that followed, whenever Thomas was at home to tuck in the little ones, his brothers and sisters would badger him to tell them of his adventures. Isabel would gather the family together by announcing that they were to hear "a *real* tale of a *real* knight, Sir Thomas, Knight of the Realm."

Then Thomas would tell his story, always remembering to end it like all good dragon tales . . .

"As was the way, it was done."

The End

Acknowledgments

Thomas and the Dragon Queen was a gift. The words flowed like a torrent from my heart onto the page at a time when I was stuck on other projects that did not seem to be going anywhere. Yes, it was a gift—but it was an unruly one that needed to be tucked in here, expanded a bit there, and polished throughout. To do that, I relied upon the help and support of a good number of friends and critics. My grateful thanks go out to: Sam Ehnis-Clark, my grandson and middle-school-age reader, for his thoughtful comments; Jack Pilutti, another young reader; my friends Ruth Haldeman, Ann Hoadley, Susan Livingston, Sherry Roberts, and Paula Schaffner; and my hardworking critique group of Valerie Carey, B.J. Connor, Tracy Gallup, Mary Lind, Deb Pilutti, Jacqui Robbins, Ginny Ryan, Nancy Shaw, Shanda Trent, and Hope Vestergaard. Finally, I must acknowledge my husband and first reader, "Sir" Gerald Clark, for continuing to be my guiding light, and my editor, Michelle Frey, who unreservedly allowed *Thomas* to steal her heart.

About the Author

SHUTTA CRUM writes books for children and poetry for adults. She is also a storyteller, a lecturer, and a librarian. In 2005, she was honored by being one of eight authors invited to the White House for the annual Easter Egg Roll. She was born in Paintsville, Kentucky, and now lives on a farm in Ann Arbor, Michigan.